An Illustrated Death

AN ILLUSTRATED DEATH

JUDI CULBERTSON

WITNESS
IMPULSE

An Imprint of HarperCollins Publishers

This is a work of fiction. Names, characters, places, and incidents are products of the author's imagination or are used fictitiously and are not to be construed as real. Any resemblance to actual events, locales, organizations, or persons, living or dead, is entirely coincidental.

EPub Edition OCTOBER 2013 ISBN: 9780062296337
Print Edition ISBN: 9780062296344

10 9 8 7 6 5 4 3 2 1

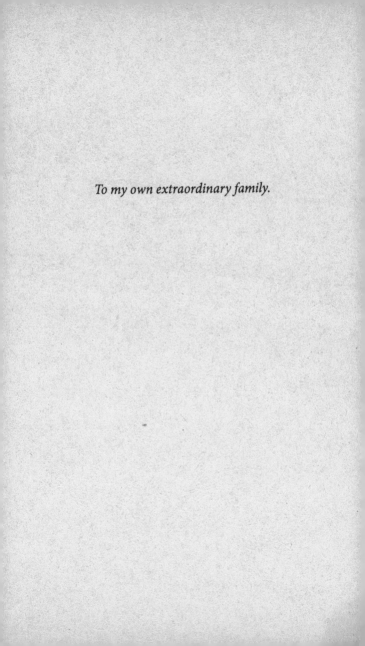

To my own extraordinary family.

ACKNOWLEDGMENTS

ONCE AGAIN THANK you to my tireless agent, Agnes Birnbaum of Bleecker Street Associates, who has gone the distance for me, and to my extraordinary editor at HarperCollins, Chelsey Emmelhainz, who knows instinctively what a book needs—Maxwell Perkins, watch out!

To my New York City writers' group, who continue to hold my feet to the fire: Jean Ayer, Myriam Chapman, Teresa Giordano, Tom House, Eleanor Hyde, Elizabeth Jakab, Maureen Sladen, Marcia Slatkin, and, most warmly, Adele Glimm for her friendship, multiple readings, and always offering a place to spend the night.

Thanks to my online booksellers' group, Bibliophile.com, for being so generous with their information.

I come from a family of writers and depend on their support and love. Here's to Tom Randall, Andy Culbertson, Robin Culbertson, John Chaffee, Heide Lange, Jessie and Joshua Chaffee, Brendan Kiely, and David Chaffee. And to the others, who love books too: David and Liz Randall, Caroline Chaffee, Dave, Katie, and Charlotte Bennett.

Finally, to the people who light up my life every day with their creativity and love: Tom, Andy, Robin, Emily, and Andrew.

Ignatz, Vladimir, and Pangur get a shout-out too.

CHAPTER ONE

THE DEAD MAN smiled up at me.

I stared back sadly. Then I read the newspaper clipping on my worktable one more time.

Illustrator, Granddaughter
Drown in Family Pool

Tragedy struck an artistic dynasty in Springs yesterday morning when Nate Erikson, 67, and Morgan Marshall, 4, drowned in a swimming pool on the grounds of the family's estate. The victims were rushed to Southampton Hospital, where efforts at resuscitation failed. A police spokesman stated that Mr. Erikson had been attempting to rescue his granddaughter, but succumbed himself.

Because I make my living selling used and rare books over the Internet, I spend a lot of time in the ancient barn behind my house, cataloging new finds and shipping them around the world. Dinnertime had come and gone but I worked on. I promised myself a spinach-goat cheese pizza and some Yellow Tail Chardonnay. Soon.

The story about Nate Erikson had lain next to my computer for the past three months.

There were the usual comparisons to N. C. Wyeth, Howard Pyle, and Norman Rockwell and a list of some of the books Nate Erikson had illustrated: *The Complete Sherlock Holmes*, Charles Dickens classics, and the better-known Shakespearean plays. Nate Erikson's survivors included five children, his widow, Eve McGready Erikson, and several other grandchildren.

Whenever I read the clipping I felt the same emptiness I'd had when John Updike and Robert Parker died. My connection to Nate Erikson went back even further, to my childhood and *Bible Stories for Good Children*. I was not a good child, but my Methodist parents took the title at face value, never noticing the wry twists Nate gave to the illustrations. Instead of the cliché image of Noah leading pairs of docile animals onto the ark, the patriarch was shown about to lose his temper with two recalcitrant lion cubs. Isaac was pictured after the sacrifice attempt, looking at the knife in his father's hand with disbelief.

Care for another walk up the mountain, son?
You're kidding, right, Dad?

My parents suspected nothing until they found my twin sister, Patience, and me trying to raise our little brother from the dead.

"*Don't breathe,*" *Patience commanded.* "*Don't breathe until I say, 'Lazarus, come forth!'*"

"*Jon, I can see your stomach moving,*" *I accused.*

Bible Stories for Good Children disappeared from the room we shared.

When I became a bookseller, the first thing I did was track down a replacement copy of *Bible Stories*. I was always on the lookout for Nate Erikson's books and tomorrow I would have the chance to buy more at a sale that had almost slipped by me. Another book dealer had mentioned it when we were standing in line at an estate sale that morning waiting for the doors to open.

"Are you going to the sale at the Nate Erikson house tomorrow?"

"What sale? I didn't see any ads," I said.

"I hear they only sent invitations to bookstores."

So what was I? Granted, I sold books over the Internet instead of owning a brick-and-mortar shop and I wasn't listed in the yellow pages, but still . . .

I felt torn between outrage that his family was getting rid of his books so soon and hope that I would be able to own some of them.

Self-interest won.

CHAPTER TWO

THE SALE AT the Erikson estate was the Saturday after Labor Day, late in the book-buying season. When I studied the ads in *Newsday* that Friday night over my belated pizza, I found no other sales in the Hamptons, though there were one or two closer to where I lived. Most of the listings were for Nassau County, nearer New York City. But it didn't matter. Missing a sale at Nate Erikson's home was like passing up dinner at the White House because you preferred Taco Bell.

Although the sale did not start until 9 a.m., I set my alarm for dawn. I needed time to feed the cats, Raj and Miss T, and stop at the all-night coffee shop, Qwikjava, for the largest cup they sold. Most of all, I had to make sure that my ten-year-old van would start. To miss one of the most promising sales of the decade because of a dead battery would be beyond tragic.

As it was, the trip to the Erikson estate took longer

than I'd expected. Light was erasing the sky's blackboard by the time I veered onto Springs–Fireplace Road. I sped by the Jackson Pollock homestead, going so fast that I missed the turn onto Cooper's Farm Lane. Backing up I knocked down an old wooden fence. Someone would have to put it up again.

Next to the tasteful "Estate Sale" sign was another that made me smile. The name "Adam's Revenge" was painted in dark green letters inside a border of flowers, a grinning serpent peeping out from behind a red hibiscus. No doubt the name was meant to express Adam's hope of creating a better Garden of Eden than the one from which he had been ejected.

Then the house came into view, an imposing, five-gabled structure with a wraparound porch. The salt air had turned its shingles silver gray, making a nice contrast to the turquoise shutters. Like the sign, the house was bordered by flowers, remnants of the summer: impatiens, begonias, and roses, with a few fat blue hydrangeas hanging on.

The road ended in a gravel circle and I braked abruptly, scattering pebbles. But—damn! Why were so many cars already here? It was barely 6 a.m. If even half the drivers had passengers, I might as well turn around and go home. I would never be in the first ten. Ten was the magic number, the number of people allowed inside when the doors opened. Everyone else had to wait until one of the first came out before the next was allowed in. By then the best stuff was gone.

Stepping into the September air, I got a whiff of the

marshes of Napeague Bay and looked around to find out who was handing out numbers. The first dealer to arrive was usually responsible for creating the numbers system, writing them consecutively on slips of paper. This way no one could question that he was number one. Numbers were sacrosanct. The most ruthless dealers lined up meekly in one-two-three order. I had never seen anyone try to cut the line and live to tell about it.

A sleek black Lincoln had its window rolled down so I headed toward it, though I didn't recognize the car. The driver looked a cut above the usual book dealers who wore strange clothing combinations and were often missing teeth. This dealer had a gracefully arched nose, perfect silver hair, and an expensive golf shirt.

With a weary smile he handed me a slip of paper through the window.

I stared at the number: thirteen. "Oh, no! Don't tell me I came all the way out here for nothing. How could this happen?" Why hadn't I left the house an hour earlier? Why hadn't I gotten here the night before and pitched a tent in the driveway?

"Oh, please. Don't look at me like your dog's just been run over." He held out a well-manicured hand for the slip. When he returned the slip to me, the number had magically changed into a nine. "Someone from Canio's Books was supposed to be here, but they know the rules as well as anyone."

I looked at the slip again to make sure it hadn't changed back. "Thanks so much. I really appreciate it." More seemed indicated, but instinct told me he thought he would have less competition from someone who looked like me than from the preeminent bookseller of Sag Harbor.

I gave him the bad news. "I'm Delhi Laine from Secondhand Prose."

"You're a dealer?" Surprised, he took in my morning-tangled hair and my "Shakespeare Did It with a Quill" T-shirt. My jeans were dusty, and I never wore makeup this early in the morning. Most days I never got around to it at all. When you're fortysomething and working frantically to stay afloat while keeping your younger children from falling out of the lifeboat, and your husband has gone off in search of a better muse, you tend to stick to the basics.

I had been too young, a sophomore in college, when Colin Fitzhugh enticed me into sharing his life as an archeologist and poet. We had been married more than half my lifetime when he'd decided last October that I was a drag on his free spirit. Jane, Hannah, and Jason were already away in college or working and I found myself on my own for the first time. After the initial tears and disbelief, I began creating a new life. I'm still working at it.

The man in the car laughed, either at my business name or his own miscalculation. "And here I thought you were just another pretty face. Charles Tremaine. Manhattan."

"Wow." No wonder he looked like he was headed for his yacht.

"And Amagansett," he confessed. "It was only a short drive this morning."

"Ah. What do you know about this sale?"

"Very little. Word is, the family moved some books

out to the garage to get rid of them. Not Nate's books though."

"Really? Not his books?" That was a blow. I had taken all the cash I had out of the bank, planning to buy as many as I could. I knew they would sell well if I could bear to part with any.

"There hasn't been enough buzz. Buyers would be lined up like Black Friday, people from out of state if it was his library. *You* would never have gotten in. Imagine the association copies alone."

We paused in reverent silence, as if inside St. Patrick's Cathedral, and thought about the books inscribed to Nate from other famous people. The best association copy I ever had was an art catalog inscribed by Andy Warhol to Norman Mailer. It had sold on eBay for a small fortune.

"*Excuse me*, can I get a *number*?" a voice behind me interrupted. I stepped out of his way and went back to my van.

THE TROUBLE WITH important sales is that once you arrive hours early to get a good number, you have to wait around for the doors to actually open. It was too early for me to catch up on phone calls and I was too keyed up to nap. Sometimes I'll leave to get breakfast, but I'm terrified they'll decide to start the sale early. ("We have enough people here. Let's do it!") Mostly I sit in the van and read or swap war stories with other dealers. Today, though, I didn't see anyone I wanted to talk to, so I walked slowly back to my van.

For a long time I sat and stared out at the September landscape, *Let the Great World Spin* unspun on my lap. Could Charles Tremaine be right? Had I come all this way for nothing? No, it wouldn't be nothing. Just being in the atmosphere where Nate had created his magical illustrations and buying books that belonged to his family was more exciting than anything else I had scheduled for today. The plane I thought was bound for Paris had been rerouted to Miami, but a trip was still a trip.

I slid the book off my lap and climbed out of my van to look around, being careful to stay in the gravel circle. Adam's Revenge was imposing, the kind of estate featured in *Architectural Digest*. What would be like to live here? Behind the main house, the property sloped gently in all directions. I could see two Swiss chalets, a one-room schoolhouse, and a barn set farther back. It looked as if someone had airlifted an alpine village onto eastern Long Island farmland.

But where was the pool Nate and his granddaughter had drowned in? I looked around discreetly, but saw no water anywhere. Had they filled it in already, and covered it over with sod? I wouldn't blame them if they had. It would have been a horrible reminder of the two lives lost, one a little girl. A hot, honeysuckle morning in June, a golden day's promise, and then—I was ambushed by the memory of another little girl. A summer afternoon, another life forever lost. I ordered myself not to think about it now.

That door had been slammed shut nineteen years ago and I was not going to open it.

CHAPTER THREE

WHEN CHARLES TREMAINE stepped out of his Town Car and moved down the hill toward the silver gray building, other dealers were on him like butter on bread. Most carried empty cardboard boxes which they hoped to fill with treasure. I had my two vinyl boat bags tucked under one arm, my money hidden in my jeans front pocket to leave my hands free. We couldn't have been more excited than if we were lining up for Shangri-La. I didn't believe Charles's dismal prediction that we were headed for Newark instead.

Judging from the Model-T weathervane on its roof, the building had probably been a stable, then a garage. It had not been well-maintained. The green paint was peeling from its oversized window frames, and one of the panes had a long vertical crack. Dealers took turns peering in, but the windows were too dusty to see anything but long tables of books.

Back on the gravel path we sorted ourselves into one-two-three order. Except for me, the other buyers today were men. I recognized Marty Campagna talking earnestly to Charles Tremaine. *Of course*. Marty was always one of the first three in line at good sales. Rumor had it that he paid someone to stand in his place overnight.

Today he wore a red T-shirt advertising "Joey's Cadillac Repair." His black-framed glasses were duct-taped at the bridge of his nose, his cheeks stubbly. Although Marty was tall and well-muscled, I knew his brawn came more from leaping over furniture to grab prize books than from workouts at Planet Fitness. But it didn't matter how he looked, he had that elusive gift known as *Finger-Spitzengefuhl*, the tingling in his fingers that comes whenever a rare book is nearby. I didn't know if *Finger-Spitzengefuhl* was real or not. I was still waiting for mine to kick in.

MARTY HAD WASTED his money if he had paid to reserve a spot here. Once we were inside and had a chance to examine what had been laid out on the tables, I saw that Charles Tremaine was right. Someone in the family was a Danielle Steel fan. Someone else was parting with a stack of mathematics textbooks. I raced up and down the long plank tables to make sure, but there were no art books, no Erikson-illustrated volumes at all.

Yet the sale wasn't a total loss. From underneath a table I pulled out a grimy carton of older first editions still in dust jackets: *The Bean Trees, The Circus of Dr. Lao, The Heart Is a Lonely Hunter.* And—yes—two Ayn Rands! I didn't even stop to see if the books were inscribed, just shoved them into my green-and-white vinyl bag. A dust jacket can increase a book's value by up to ninety percent. Ayn Rand, like Mozart, never went out of style.

I was moving toward the cash table to pay when Marty stepped into my path. "Hey, Blondie. Find anything good?" He reached down and rummaged through my bag, dislodging books to see what was at the bottom. I held my breath. More than once he had examined my stash, seen something he wanted, and tried to force me to sell the book to him.

Today he jerked back his hand as if to avoid contamination. "*Dreck.*"

"No, it's not." I felt a moment of doubt, then remembered the Ayn Rands in dust jackets.

"Know what I bought? Three books. What a waste!"

Then why are you hanging around?

"I need to talk to you." Evidently his *Finger-Spitzengefuhl* extended to reading minds. "Naw, too complicated. I'll call you later."

And he was off to another sale.

When I reached the gravel area, the dust from the ancient Cadillac Marty drove had long settled. Instead a young woman sat off to the side in a director's chair, arms crossed. A lanky, bespectacled man stood protectively behind her. *Nate Erikson's children?* They were definitely a matched set: gingery hair, pale freckled skin, high aristocratic noses. They had the look of money—her peach sweater was cashmere, her designer jeans fashionably white at the knees. His plaid flannel shirt and Levi's had a deliberately worn-out air that hadn't come from shooting deer.

They studied me, then exchanged a look.

If I had been anywhere but the Hamptons, I might have been worried.

"Hey there!" the woman called, as if I were her neighbor's pet dog.

"Hi."

She pushed up from the canvas seat and the pair edged closer.

"Are you a book dealer?" he demanded.

"Yes." I had run into owners who were hostile to professionals, the last time a month ago. As I left a tag sale carrying a stack of profusely illustrated books on Wedgwood china, a woman in a denim skirt had stopped me.

"How much did you pay for those?" she'd asked.

I could tell from the pinched look of her eyes and mouth that my acquisitions had once been hers.

I should have made up something, but I'd told her the truth.

"That's all you paid? I hope you feel good, profiting from someone else's tragedy."

I started to offer her more money, then realized that no amount would be enough to make things right for her. Still I could not shake my guilt, though I told myself that if I hadn't bought those books, someone else would have. *Sure.* Like rationalizing it was okay to wear a fur coat because those particular animals were already dead.

I reminded myself that the Eriksons had sought out bookstore owners.

"Do you assess books too?" he wanted to know.

"Yes."

"You can tell how valuable—"

"What did you think of these books?" she interrupted him, pointing to my bag.

What could I say that wouldn't insult someone they were related to?

"Well, I bought some."

Her pale blue eyes probed my face. "Were they what you wanted?"

Another trick question. "Not what I was hoping for, maybe, but I did find some good fiction. No art books though."

"No. That's what we want to talk to you about." She looked at the man and he nodded. "We need someone to appraise my father's books. His library is good, but we need to know how good."

Be still, my heart. It was a dream I hadn't known I had. "I could do that." Yet a part of myself asked, *Why me?* Why not Charles Tremaine or someone who looked like an authority? I knew they had invited only professional booksellers, perhaps for that reason, but something about it made less than perfect sense.

"What's your fee?" plaid-shirt demanded.

My fee? "Forty-five dollars an hour." That sounded like a lot of money for something I would have done for nothing. Just to have the opportunity to look at Nate Erikson's books . . .

"Forty-five dollars?" The woman sounded scandalized. "Mechanics get *ninety*-five an hour. Lawyers are over three hundred!"

"Plus gas and expenses," I added hastily.

She laughed then, a clear note that carried out over the early September landscape. "Fifty-five dollars an hour, none of this nickel-and-dime stuff. When can you start?"

I made myself breathe. "Monday?"

"Fine. Come around nine. I'm Bianca Erikson, by the way, and this is my brother, Claude. The books—"

"How long do you think it will take you to tell us what they're worth?" he interrupted. "This horse has to run."

"Well—it depends on how many there are."

"We have no idea," Bianca said. "They're in his studio covered in dust. The door's been padlocked since the day it happened."

"The studio's been locked since the accident?" It came out before I could censor it.

She rounded on both of us. "Why does everyone keep saying what happened was an accident? It was no damn accident!"

Claude made a protesting sound in his throat.

Bianca gave her brother a scornful look, her eyes as pale and hard as my amethyst birthstone. "Go on, just sweep it under the rug like everything else." Then she strode away, pushing the director's chair over backward as she went.

Claude righted the chair quickly. "I don't know why she says crazy things like that," he muttered. "Even the autopsy said they drowned." He started down the hill after her.

If this had been a Nate Erikson illustration, a serpent would have peered out of the bushes with a quizzical look.

CHAPTER FOUR

I DROVE AWAY feeling lightheaded, either because I would be spending time with Nate Erikson's books *and* getting paid, or because it was nearly ten o'clock and I had not yet eaten anything. I decided to stop for a bagel and cream cheese, something I could eat on my way to the next sale.

More than anything, I was shocked by what Bianca Erikson had said. If what happened wasn't an accident, what were the choices? Surely a man with Nate's talent and sensibilities would not have committed suicide, much less drowned his own granddaughter. Even if in despair, I couldn't imagine him inflicting that pain on his family.

That left murder.

Yet as Claude Erikson had pointed out, the police had been satisfied. Something else occurred to me: Had it been *her* daughter who drowned? Maybe Bianca was unable to accept the fact that life was so precarious that a single moment of inattention could have fatal and permanent results.

Tell me about it.

I DECIDED TO stop at the sale closest to home, along an unpaved country road in Shoreham. The ad had emphasized the large amount of craft supplies, so I wasn't expecting much in the way of books. If there was still a line, I wouldn't even wait. But there was no crowd at the front door and I walked right in. I bypassed balls of colored wool and paint tubes twisted into odd shapes, and found some books on the basement shelves. I knew to look for small publishers and esoteric subjects, detailed explanations of weaving techniques or lithographic processes. *100 Sock Monkeys You Can Make* wasn't on my list.

Not that there was anything *wrong* with sock puppets, I assured an imaginary mob of angry craftspeople. During the years when I'd followed Colin around the globe to guest lectureships and archeological digs, I often had to educate the kids myself. We did leaf rubbings and identified rocks, wrote stories and learned pottery-making at kivas. In England, I took photographs of the countryside and hand-colored them. I would have kept doing that if . . .

I wasn't a born craftsperson anyway. My real passion had been reading, whenever and wherever I could. A memory: Colin coming in sweaty and tired after a long day and the kids wild and shrieking. His exasperated command: "Put down that book and make dinner!"

"I'm tired of cooking. Let's phone out for Chinese."

"Delhi, we're in the middle of the Chihuahuan Desert!"

I knew that. I was only teasing. In the next moment I'd relent, and jump up and kiss him. He'd shower, and we'd end up sitting in camp chairs drink icy Dos Equis, watching the tangerine sunset play on the ruffles of sand. Sometimes we clasped hands as he described his day and the children played quietly at our feet.

Memories, memories.

I didn't seriously get into bookselling until my parents died. My sister, Patience, didn't want their collection of books cluttering up her Manhattan apartment or beach house, and my brother, Jon, in Hollywood, was too busy making movies like *Poisoned Carrots* to want a retired minister's library. So I brought the books home, along with the faded Oriental rugs that are now on the barn floor. I didn't know what to do with so many books, so I started selling them online. That's how I discovered what I was born to do.

AT TODAY'S SALE in Shoreham, I found several advanced quilting books and a few on watercolor that showed interesting techniques. I had been back in the barn for about an hour describing the day's finds for the Internet—*Atlas Shrugged* was a true first edition in great condition and I listed the book for four hundred dollars—when the phone rang. I answered it cheerfully, as I did no matter my mood. "Secondhand Prose!"

"Meet me at the Old Frigate."

"Marty?"

I was only trying to identify the voice, but he took the question as a challenge. "*What?*"

"Why there?"

"Because it's mine now."

"What do you mean? You bought the Old Frigate?"

"Be there in five minutes."

"I can't—"

But I was explaining that I had too much work to do to a dial tone.

PORT LEWIS IS an old whaling village, one of a number that make up Long Island's North Shore. The village has a natural harbor and quaint setting, but it came late to the party. When we first moved here, Port Lewis was dominated by a Salvation Army thrift shop and a seafood restaurant whose proprietor was always drunk, making it a source of pride if he let you in to eat. The grocery store had sawdust-covered wooden floors back then. But one summer when we were at a dig in Peru, Farm Foods was replaced by The Gap. Now we had You're Worth It! Day Spa, five nautical gift stores, and an English tea room. There were rumors about a taxidermy shop soon to open, though I couldn't imagine what kind of tourists that would attract.

I parked in the residents-only lot and walked slowly up the street. After the murder of the Old Frigate owner, Margaret Weller, people had started leaving flowers and stuffed toys with literary themes—Babar, Madeleine, and Winnie-the-Pooh—crammed up against the bookshop door. I dreaded seeing the remnants. Margaret had been my best friend.

I was relieved to see that Marty had cleared everything away. "The Old Frigate" was still painted in gold script on the glass, but the front windows were bare. Seeing its nakedness, I was overtaken by a sense of desolation. I had loved the bookshop with its look of a British men's club, its fireplace, the leather sofa and paisley wing chairs, the Oriental rugs. You could get lost for hours, and sometimes in winter, when book sales were few, I had. How could something so wonderful have gone so wrong?

Marty, still wearing his red "Cadillac Repair" T-shirt and stained khakis, unlocked the door. "Come in, come in!"

He actually reached out and grabbed my arm to pull me inside, then locked the door again as if hordes of people were clamoring to get in.

Unwillingly, I looked around. The beautiful oak shelves were empty, but the chairs and brown leather sofa still surrounded the fireplace. Even the small photograph of Emily Dickinson, who had inspired the bookshop's name by writing, "There is no frigate like a book to bear us lands away," still hung beside the door. My eyes flickered over to the marble fireplace hearth.

"I had a cleaning service in, got rid the blood." Marty assured me. "I hired fumigators too, the basement smelled like rotten—"

"Don't!" I remembered that nauseating stench, like

meat left out in the sun for days. Margaret had still been in the hospital after being attacked. I had been the one to discover her assistant Amil's body jammed and rotting in a downstairs closet.

"Yeah, right. So sit down."

"I can't stay—" But the shop was already pulling me in. *Sit here*, my favorite wing chair urged. *Have you forgotten us already?*

I ignored my favorite chair and perched on the edge of a leather love seat. "I can't believe you bought this. There was a huge balloon loan coming due."

"Popped it," Marty said smugly, pushing up his taped glasses. "The place is mine, free and clear. All those years Margaret had it, I was dying to make something of it. The moment I heard it was for sale, ka-boom."

I tend to forget that Marty can afford anything he wants. When Suffolk County was still farmland, his grandfather arrived with a cesspool-pumping truck and, impatient with how long the process took, he created a faster waste-dissolving substance. Mario Campagna's timing was perfect. He sold the patent to a national manufacturer, and guaranteed the family fortune. You can still see a few of the original Campagna trucks on the road with their slogan, "We turn your waste into gold!" along with a drawing of a mischievous little king perched on a toilet.

Marty was one of the first booksellers I met when I started going to sales. He was already legendary: He had picked up his first book at a rummage sale for a quarter—a book that turned out to be a signed copy of Jack Kerouac's

first novel. I noticed him because he seemed to know exactly where in the house to head the moment the doors
opened. Marty would be stacking valuable books in cartons while I still stood in the hallway, wondering where
to start. I'd been attracted to his confidence, but put off
by his bulldozer approach.

"What are you going to do with the shop?" I asked.

"Do with it? This place is a class act. It's a perfect venue
to sell the books I don't have collectors lined up for. I've
been getting into art lately, buying up old paintings. They
can go in here too. And that"—he made his finger into a
gun and cocked it at me—"is where *you* come in."

The gesture was so unlike Marty, who scorned anything affected, that I realized he was nervous about what
he was going to say.

"You're good with people, Blondie. People like you.
And you know your books."

And? It took me a moment to understand. "You want
me to run the Old Frigate?"

"I'd change the name, of course. It would be a higher-
end shop."

"But what about my business?" How could I run his
bookshop full-time and still keep up with Secondhand
Prose?

He waved that away. "Internet selling is *so* over. You'll
make a lot more money working for me."

I stared at him. In a New York minute he had erased
my reason for getting up in the morning. He had made
Secondhand Prose into a hobby, something like crochet-

ing scarves for boutiques. No, not even that, since I didn't make the books—only scavenged them.

The most insulting part was that he hadn't *meant* to be insulting. He hadn't suggested I sell my books here either. No doubt they would compromise his high-end shop. Worst of all, what he said about the Internet was true. The golden days of online bookselling were over, the prices on the book sites eroding for years. Several years ago an army of amateurs had marched in, pricing perfectly good books for under a dollar. Nobody in my dealers' group, BookEm.com, could figure out how such sellers made any money. Maybe they didn't. Now *there* was a hobby for you.

Marty also held a card he didn't know he possessed. My living situation was precarious. My husband, Colin, in his position as archeology professor at Stony Brook University, was the reason I could live cheaply in the university-owned farmhouse and barn. If he decided to make our separation permanent, I would have to move. I had been shocked when he left, and he was still calling the shots. Where would I find a place I could afford that could hold eight thousand books? If I didn't accept Marty's offer, I might be forced to work nights at McDonald's.

I looked past Marty to the beautiful, now forlorn, bookshop I had once loved. It could be brought back to life—of course it could. I saw myself decorating the shop windows with books and antiques for special occasions, discussing literature with the collectors who stopped by. I loved to talk about books, and Marty's were the kind of treasures that other shops kept locked in glass cases. At the annual open house, I would be the one offering cups of champagne punch and smoked salmon hors d'oeuvres. I would be—finally—respectable in Colin's eyes. Maybe he would decide I was worthy of him.

I gave my head a shake to clear it. What was I thinking? I had fallen under Marty's spell just like the Little Match Girl had been enticed by the flames in the matches she struck. When the glorious visions faded, I would be left in the dark and cold too.

"Well, it's something to think about."

Wrong answer. Marty looked surprised—and displeased.

You need to work on your people skills, buddy.

"Better not take too long," he warned.

Or what? The worst that could happen would be that he would find someone else to run his shop, and I would be left to my own bliss.

CHAPTER FIVE

MONDAY MORNING'S SKY was as dingy and rumpled as the bed I'd left behind. The September sun would burn through by noon, giving the fall landscape the golden light of a Maxfield Parrish illustration, but my ride out to Springs was gray. On the other hand, who cared? I had been awake since 5 a.m., too excited about Nate Erikson's books to sleep any longer, and equally worried too about my ability to do them justice. Although I'd attended the Colorado Antiquarian Booksellers Seminar twice and spent the last five years assessing books daily, I had never done a formal appraisal. I made sure that my laptop, my trusted deputy, was in its black canvas case beside me.

Pausing for the red light on Bridgehampton's main street, it occurred to me that the Eriksons might not have wi-fi. I'd been to sales this far out on Long Island where they couldn't get a signal for credit card machines. I had an image of myself staying up late every night, confirming book values once I was home.

One more thing to obsess about.

Bianca Erikson was waiting for me on the gravel driveway unsmiling, her arms crossed. Today she was dressed in a navy-striped jersey and expensive slacks, her hair tied back with a navy-and-gold checked scarf. Her prominent nose kept her from being conventionally pretty, but her face was that of a wealthy young duchess.

Was the appraisal off? Was I *late*? I glanced at my dashboard clock, but 9 a.m. was the time we had agreed on.

"Hello," she called, walking over to my van. The blue "Got Books?" logo on the dented white front door seemed to amuse her. "I wondered if you'd actually come."

"Why not?"

"Well, most help shows up at *their* own convenience—if they bother showing up at all. You should see the trouble we have getting someone to do the weeding!"

The weeding? Did she really equate me with a Guatemalan day worker?

"Anyway, the cover story is that you're here to illustrate my book of children's poems."

I grabbed for a part of the sentence I understood. "You write poetry?"

"I've had three chapbooks published. Chapbooks are what they call little books of poems."

Oh, really? Evidently she had forgotten that I was a book dealer. She didn't know that my husband was the poet Colin Fitzhugh, so didn't know that I had spent too many years buried alive under those precious little volumes. One of Colin's chapbooks, *Voices We Don't Want to Hear*, had been shortlisted for a National Book Award.

"All I mean is, we need an explanation for my mother as to why you're here. She'd be upset if she knew anyone was touching my father's precious books. She wants the studio left exactly as it was when he was alive."

"Who do the books belong to now?"

It seemed a reasonable question, but Bianca looked as if I'd caught her cheating at golf. "You have to understand something if this is going to work. My mother hasn't been herself for a while. She's been worse since it happened, so it's easier if she doesn't know about you. When we walk down to my cottage, we'll be blocked by trees and can go into the studio through the back door. Oh, good—you've brought a professional-looking bag."

We both looked at my black laptop case, and I remembered my earlier fears. "Is there wi-fi?"

"Are you kidding? We're probably providing Internet for all of Springs. My brother Puck had a very strong signal installed."

Puck? Another escapee from Stratford-upon-Avon.

I followed Bianca down a grassy path. I should have known there would be a catch. Things were never straightforward for people like me. The only contest I had ever won, writing an essay on forest fire prevention, was because I was the only entrant. Did I really want to be here under false pretenses? "What about the rest of the family? Do they know why I'm here?" I asked.

Now she looked as if I had just rammed her with my

shopping cart. "Of course. You met Claude. This was a group decision, except for Mama. We'll probably have to remind her who you are every day."

Why would I be seeing Mama every day?

When we got closer to one of the white chalets, Bianca said, "My father had these built for us so we would never leave. No one did, except for my sister who's out of the picture. Speaking of pictures, don't touch any of the paintings!"

I felt like I was on a school trip. "What if I want to touch up a few of them during my lunch hour?"

She didn't get the joke. "You won't have time."

"The help doesn't get lunch?"

Now she did smile. "I mean, you'll be eating with us."

"That's okay, you don't have to feed me."

"No, you *have* to be there, you're my collaborator. I've already told Mama about you, she'll be suspicious if you don't eat with us."

I glanced at my work clothes: jeans and a faded red Cornell sweatshirt from my younger daughter, Hannah. I had planned to escape back to Sunrise Highway and relax with a book and a strawberry shake. If I'd known I'd be trading bon mots with the Eriksons, I'd have listened to *Morning Edition*.

Finally we were outside Nate Erikson's studio, a two-story building with the same silvery shingles as those on the house. I wondered why I hadn't noticed it on Saturday, then realized that my view had been blocked by the garage. We went around to the back door, which was painted the deep green of the fir trees on the property behind us. Strips of paint had turned brittle and started to pull away, and I resisted the urge to reach out and rip one off completely.

Bianca twisted a key into the lock, then handed it to me. "Don't lose it."

"Why don't you keep it?"

"No. If I need to get in there's a key in the pantry. Anyone can use it—not that anyone does. Growing up we were never allowed inside the studio." She gave the door a small push. "I'll come get you at one."

And I would be meeting Nate Erikson's family.

CHAPTER SIX

I STEPPED OVER the threshold, into the studio of one of America's best-loved illustrators. There should have been organ music, a beam of heavenly light illuminating the wooden floor. At the least, a mounted camera to make sure I didn't steal anything. I breathed in the dry smell of summer attics as I patted the wall for a light switch, relieved that there was no scent of damp or mildew. Mildew is a death sentence for books.

When I flipped a toggle, lights came on everywhere, but were strongest over the worktable. Its rough wooden surface held coffee cans jammed with brushes and half-used tubes of paint in jagged rows. Serious-looking magnifying glasses had their own container. There was even, eerily, a white china coffee cup, matching breakfast plate, and neatly folded napkin still in place. Like Miss Haversham's parlor, waiting for someone who would never come back to use it.

Automatically, I glanced toward the door. When no ghostly hand opened it, I set my case gingerly on the table, feeling like I was in a museum display. It seemed sacrilegious to sit in Nate's metal, high-backed chair, and I half expected a guard to rush over and order me out. But it was the only seat in the work area.

The wall behind me, which faced south, was made of large windows, now covered by black drapes. The long wall opposite held tall art bins with each canvas in its own stall like a Thoroughbred pony. Those paintings had to be worth a fortune. Norman Rockwell's cover painting for the *Saturday Evening Post*, *Breaking Home Ties*, had sold at auction in 2006 for over fifteen million dollars.

If the family needed money, why hadn't they sold a couple of these? Then I remembered the widow's insistence on leaving everything just as it was.

At the far end of the room were stairs to a loft that circled the perimeter of the studio. The opposite side held a fireplace and several faded chairs. Nearby were bookcases holding plumed hats, golden crowns, pith helmets, and other accessories needed for historic verisimilitude. Gowns, velvet waistcoats, and army garb were squeezed indiscriminately together on a long metal clothes rack. When Nate Erikson started illustrating, the Internet was not around for reference.

All I needed now were the books.

They had to be up in the loft. I climbed the stairs and

stepped into a cloud of dust motes sparkling in the light. But at least there were hundreds of books here, housed in tall shelves facing each other. From downstairs all you could see were the bookcases' wooden backs.

I walked up and down, my fingers gently touching spines, but no *Finger-Spitzengefuhl* kicked in to guide me. I did see that they were shelved in chronological order and decided to begin with Nate Erikson's earliest work. I pulled out as many books as I could carry and brought them to the table downstairs. Next I set up my laptop. When my e-mail loaded instantly, I realized that the signal was strong indeed.

Nate had begun his career in the time-honored way by accepting any assignment he was offered, starting with a short-lived series about a boy explorer in the Arctic, a collection of dog stories, and two minor novels of Zane Grey. Although the stories were forgettable, these books had been published in small print runs before Nate Erikson was famous, making them more valuable than his later best sellers. The illustrations were vividly colored, but had an impressionistic quality not typical of his later work. I wondered when his style had changed.

BY LATE MORNING, I could no longer resist looking at the paintings the illustrations were based on. I informed the imaginary museum guard that looking at them was part of my research, that I was not touching anything I shouldn't—not really—then went over to the wooden bins and started removing canvases carefully. They weren't large, perhaps twenty-four inches by thirty-six inches, and spanned Nate's whole career. I was delighted to see the painting of the Israelites crossing the Red Sea from my storybook, a baby looking wide-eyed over his mother's shoulder at the Egyptian soldiers as they started to drown.

The next canvas caught on something. I wiggled the edge back and forth, then gave a tug—and was horrified to hear a ripping sound. I had ripped a Nate Erikson canvas! I had destroyed a museum masterpiece. I might as well have gone to the Met and slashed Monet's *Water Lilies*. No wonder Bianca Erikson had warned me not to touch anything. She had known from looking at me that I was not reliable.

My instinct was to push the picture back into its slot, and pretend that I had never gone near this part of the studio. But I had to see what I had done. I slipped my arm in as far as I could and, with a sinking heart, tried to remove a canvas that had gotten caught on a nail. How much damage had I caused? Would it take everything I earned here for its restoration? Maybe I would be making restitution for the rest of my life.

I finally worked the painting free, and stared at it, confused. It was no book illustration. It was a nude of a young woman with a large black X obliterating her face. Someone had crisscrossed her breasts with a knife as well, leaving hanging triangles. It was one of these flaps that had gotten snagged.

Thank you, Lord. I had not destroyed a priceless painting. It was hardly a masterpiece and it had already been ruined. Had Nate even painted it? If he had, why would he mutilate his own work? Yet Bianca had told me no one else had been allowed in the studio. I studied the painting more carefully. There was something familiar about the tangled waves of light hair that fell past her shoulders.

Belatedly I realized the hair was just like mine.

CHAPTER SEVEN

A KNOCK ON the studio door brought me out of the Old West. I looked at my watch and saw, surprised, that it was after one.

"Did you think I'd forgotten you?" Bianca said when I pulled back the door. "I got a phone call just as I was leaving that I had to take."

She had changed her clothes and was wearing tan slacks, a pin-striped cotton blouse, and chunky gold jewelry. Her crinkly red hair had been released from the scarf and was held behind her ears by tortoiseshell combs.

"I brought you a clean shirt in case you wanted to change." She held out a white waffle-weave cotton sweater with navy and red stripes highlighting the V-neck. It looked like it had been ordered from a Talbots catalog and I couldn't imagine myself wearing it. That's the thing about us non-fashionistas. We look as if we'd wear anything. But we won't.

"I can wear something else tomorrow and meet your family then."

She took another look at my red sweatshirt with its grinning Cornell bear and shook her head. "No, you're fine. You're supposed to be an artist. You should see what some of our other guests used to come to table in."

Come to table? Was this a meal or a coronation? "What did Andy Warhol wear?"

"Oh, he never came here. My father thought he would be a bad influence on us. My father was very careful about who we were exposed to. We didn't even go to school." She seemed proud of that.

"Isn't that against the law?"

"Oh, we had tutors. The schools around here were terrible anyway, all Bonacker families."

Bonacker was the traditional name for the farmers and baymen who had settled Springs back in the 1600s and 1700s. The fact that names like Miller and King were revered by historical societies, did not seem to impress Bianca. "My father thought school was a waste of time, even college. Vietnam was his art institute."

OUTSIDE THE DAY had already started to perk up, a thin gold line outlining the trees and clouds. After a steamy summer, the cooler air felt wonderful. But as soon as I thought that, I started to feel sweaty. What was I doing, invading this family's world? Less than three months ago they had suffered a terrible double loss. I couldn't imagine why they would want to entertain a stranger and wondered if the parents of the dead child would be there.

I followed Bianca up the front stairs into a dark-paneled hall covered with paintings. I recognized Fairfield Porter, Ben Shahn, and other artists and hoped that the family had a good alarm system. Below the artwork were dark brown wicker chairs with flowered cushions and the kind of undistinguished rugs you might see in a hunting lodge. That was what the room reminded me of, I realized, one of those lakeside vacation homes that upstate owners called "camps."

The hall turned right and opened into a dining room. With its pale blue woodwork and corner cabinets stuffed with silver, the room seemed to belong to a different house. A portrait of a young, light-haired man in a pale blue painter's smock hung over an impressive brick fireplace. He was smiling so broadly that he seemed ready to burst out of the frame. I realized it was Nate Erikson and my heart squeezed. *I don't belong here.*

At the head of a long cherry table was a woman with a pretty, finely creased face and white hair clipped back with a barrette. Several strands straggled thinly over her midnight blue turtleneck. Her sharp eyes, also blue, followed me all the way to the Windsor chair that Bianca pulled out for me.

"You're late," the matriarch, Eve Erikson, announced.

Not exactly the dithering personage Bianca had warned me about, though a dark-skinned woman in a pale green uniform hovered in the shadows behind her. A personal attendant?

Then Eve was gaping at me as if Bianca had brought in

Typhoid Mary. "What are *you* doing here? Who invited you here?"

Before I could open my mouth, several people at the table rushed to explain. Bianca prevailed. "Mama, this isn't— This is my collaborator, Delhi Laine. Remember, she's here to illustrate my *Good Night* poems."

Eve squinted at me. "You're an artist? Where did you study?"

I could sense that everyone at the table was watching, waiting to hear what I would say. But I was my parents' daughter, unable to lie. "I'm self-taught."

"No shame in that." She turned away, dismissing me.

"You've already met my brother Claudius—Claude, I mean, and this is his wife, Lynn." Bianca tipped her head toward the man at the foot of the table. Still standing, I could see that his reddish curly hair had retreated to a fringe above his ears, leaving a considerable dome. In the breast pocket of his wrinkled cotton shirt was a collection of pens and compasses, signaling a draftsman too busy to change clothes for lunch.

Lynn, with her cap of blond hair and pleasant expression, was the kind of woman I would chat with in the supermarket line.

I nodded at them.

"My other brother, Puck." Puck, across from me, tilted his head in a small salute. With his fair curly hair and wry expression, the name suited him perfectly.

Bianca and I sat down. She was unfolding her white napkin when I became aware of a rhythmic clatter of silverware. I looked over and saw that the young woman beside Puck was tapping the back of her spoon against her knife and looking at Bianca. With her head turned, I saw that her dark hair was pulled back in a long braid, and realized that she reminded me of the Indian women in Santa Fe paintings. From the top of her ear and bisecting her cheek to her chin was the kind of running scar made by stitches.

Puck's wife?

"Oh, sorry. This is my sister, Rosa." Bianca's voice was as flat as the pale mauve tablecloth.

"Hi, Rosa." I smiled at her.

But she only nodded shyly. Was she mute?

Bianca and Claude bore a strong resemblance to the portrait of Nate, Puck had his mother's Irish features, but Rosa was hard to place. The red turtleneck she had on gave an unfortunate emphasis to the roll of fat above her stomach.

I was picking up my own napkin when I realized I had forgotten to wash up, because I didn't usually when I was eating alone. I didn't even wash fruit before eating. It was only book dust, but I kept my hands in my lap.

A Caesar salad had been carefully arranged at each place setting. But before one fork stabbed one piece of romaine, everyone raised their glass of iced tea and tilted it toward a blue-and-white porcelain urn standing in the center of the table.

"To the best dad ever!"

"Always in our hearts."

They took a ceremonial sip at the exact same moment, then set down their glasses with a single thud and reached for forks.

Could Nate Erikson's ashes really be in that jar?

So glad your father could join us.

Then Mama gave a cry of alarm. "We can't start without Nate!"

Was there another brother? I looked around, but could see no vacant chair.

The uniformed attendant stepped away from the sideboard and placed a consoling hand on Mama's narrow shoulder. "Now Miss Eve, you know he went to the city today. We'll save plenty of lunch for him."

I realized, chilled, that Mama must be talking about her dead husband. But was that really so unusual? It was easy to forget for a moment when someone hadn't been gone that long.

"Are you married to another artist?" Lynn asked me, smiling as she would have over her grocery cart. "I noticed your unusual wedding band."

It wasn't exactly a wedding band, though it was on my left hand, third finger. It was wide and ornately woven, an Art Deco design that Colin and I had found in an antiques shop. Neither of us cared much for conventional rings. Now, even if I wanted to, I couldn't slide it over my knuckle.

Time for more truth. "We don't live together right now. He's an archeologist who travels a lot, he teaches at Stony Brook and writes poetry. We're still mar—"

I felt Bianca's arm bang into mine. "What's his name?"

"Colin Fitzhugh?" I don't know why it came out as a question.

Her salad fork clattered onto the plate. "You're married to *Colin Fitzhugh*?"

I turned and our eyes met, hers steel gray with accusation.

Now what had I done?

I glanced at her mother—surely Bianca should know who her collaborator's husband was. But Mama was absorbed in pushing her salad croutons into an arrangement of eyes, nose, and mouth, creating a Green Man.

Claude came alive at that. "Does he have to patent his archeological finds to keep other people from claiming them?"

"Well, he publishes his findings, but everyone knows which archeologist is working where. You can't just go in and start digging. He can't keep his finds anyway. Most countries have preservation acts and they own what you excavate."

He looked disbelieving. "Then why bother?"

"For the same reason you invent things, sweetie," Lynn said, rolling her hazel eyes at me. *Men, ya gotta love 'em.* "You want to be the first to make a discovery and get recognition for it."

"Screw recognition. Show me the money. I'm not inventing stuff for the good of mankind."

"That's for sure," Puck said.

Claude slammed down his fork. "Don't patronize me, you little weasel. That company in Japan is giving Paper Pusher very serious consideration."

Paper Pusher? It sounded like an overworked clerk. "What's Paper Pusher?"

"Well . . ." He gave me an appraising look, then decided I was too dumb to steal the idea. "The Japanese are far in advance of us in many areas. They have toilets that not only take your temperature, they can analyze your blood sugar. *My* device senses when you are finished and automatically releases five squares of bathroom tissue right into your hand. At a certain content weight, it will give you ten. There's no having to fish around for a loose end and touch toilet paper that someone else has touched. The Japanese are extremely fastidious."

"The Japanese are *bad*," Eve cried, back in the conversation. "Your father hated the Japanese, and so should you."

"That war's over, Mama," Puck said easily. "After they surrendered, Dad didn't hold a grudge. My grandfather died in the South Pacific, trying to take Chichi-Jima Island when Dad was a baby," he explained to me in a lower voice. "There may have been torture involved."

So Nate Erikson's father had died in World War II and Nate himself had fought in Vietnam. I couldn't imagine either Claude or Puck holding a gun.

We were finishing our salads when there was a clatter from the archway and a woman pushed a food cart into the room. She had on a white apron over a black turtleneck sweater and pants, and looked to be in her late sixties. The golden braids twisted across her head made her look like a merry hausfrau. They also showed she was no stranger to L'Oreal hair coloring.

When she placed a platter of bluefish and bowls of mashed potatoes and zucchini on the sideboard, my appetite spiked.

I could get used to this.

But Puck looked over at the food and groaned. "Oh, Gretchen, not fish again! Don't you know how to make anything else?"

"Get a life," Bianca scolded him. "You aren't a cute little boy anymore."

"And you like fish because?"

"It's good for me."

The woman turned and looked at him, head cocked. "No dessert for you, Master Puckie."

It was so unexpected that I started to laugh. "I love bluefish," I assured her. "Any fish that has a real flavor. Especially with mashed potatoes."

Puck rolled his eyes at me. "Suck-up."

And I worried that the conversation would be too sophisticated. That the family would be too bereaved to want to talk.

I felt as if I had been dropped into the middle of a Woody Allen movie, *Annie Hall* or *Radio Days*. I tried to think of a literary analogy, but the best I could do was the Mad Hatter's Tea Party. Yet except for the toast to the urn, it seemed to be business as usual. Bianca had mentioned another sister. Perhaps she was the one who had lost her child along with her father. Perhaps the mood was more serious when she was present.

"Thank you, Aunt Gretchen," Claude called as she left, giving Puck a disgusted shake of his head.

Aunt Gretchen? Even the servants had pet names. I imagined a legion of gardeners, chauffeurs, housekeepers, and parlor maids eating below the stairs.

On the way out, passing the painting of Nate Erikson over the fireplace, I said to Claude "Is that a self-portrait?"

"No."

I waited to hear who the artist was, but he just kept on walking.

Outside on the grass, Bianca attacked me. "Why didn't you *tell* me you were married to Colin Fitzhugh? I just thought you were—" She stopped abruptly and looked over at the oak leaves that had started to turn color.

What could she say? That she had assumed, from my shabby jeans and untamed hair, I was one of the great unwashed, one of the masses born to serve people like her? She must have thought she was in Merrie Olde England.

I took advantage of her misstep. "You said that what happened to your father wasn't an accident."

She opened her mouth, then closed it. Her coral lips were as vivid as they had been before lunch, and I realized there were some lipsticks that didn't disappear as soon as you put them on. "Did I say that? I guess I did. I just get so frustrated with my family sometimes. Claude especially is ready to move on. He doesn't seem to realize that when you lose a child you can't just 'move on.'"

"She was *your* daughter?" I heard how shocked I sounded.

"Morgan. That was her name." She jerked her head

toward the studio and we started walking. "This has been the worst year of my life. First my husband in March, and now this. Oh—shit." I turned to see what had happened and saw streams of tears running down her pale face. "I'm like a goddamn sprinkler system. Everything sets me off. It's a wonder I can even get out of bed in the morning."

"I'm so sorry." I wanted to put my arm around her, hug her shoulder, let her know how much I felt for her. Yet I sensed she didn't want to be touched.

She pulled a tissue from her pants pocket and pressed it against one eye, then the other, the way you would try and keep a wound from bleeding. "You know my book of poems? I'm writing it in her memory. For her. I don't usually write kids' poems, but—it's all that keeps me going these days." She gave a sniff, loud in the stillness, and touched the tissue to her nose. "Nights are the worst. I'll sit and go over and over it trying to figure out *how* it could have happened. Morgan hated water, we could never get her near the pool. I tried to put a bathing suit on her once and she screamed. It was as if she knew something terrible would happen."

Her words stirred an answering sadness in me, rattled the doorknob to a room that had been locked as firmly as Nate Erikson's studio, but for a lot longer.

"Do they think your father had a heart attack?"

"No. Nothing like that showed up in the autopsy. He was sixty-seven, but he had a whole health regimen, lifting weights and swimming laps before anyone else was up. Morgan liked to get up early too. Aunt Gretchen would take her for a walk or let her help in the kitchen."

Aunt Gretchen was a busy lady.

Bianca put the tissue back in her pocket. "The weirdest thing was this bruise on my father's forehead." She was more composed now, not talking about her child. "It was horrible the way—while we were waiting for the ambulance and Claude was trying to give him CPR—this dark mark started to spread across his forehead. It was like something supernatural, like a photo developing. It almost looked like a *cross*." Bianca shivered in a breeze that had kicked up out of nowhere.

The mark of Cain. Or ashes from Ash Wednesday, the symbol of repentance and loss. "How did the police explain that?"

"They didn't. I mean, they said he must have crashed into the side of the pool. That something distracted him, maybe Morgan falling in."

We had reached the bottom of the hill and she turned toward her cottage. "I didn't mean to dump all this on you, you don't even know me. It happened, it's over, and I need to accept what happened. Forget what I said."

But as with anything you are ordered not to think about, I couldn't put it out of my mind.

CHAPTER EIGHT

MONDAY NIGHTS WERE reserved for talking to my children. Although I received daily e-mails from Hannah, they were usually photographs of kittens in cute clothes looking mutinous or affirmations about the power of women friends. I was instructed to send those to *my* twelve best friends, but I deleted them instead. Jason in Santa Fe didn't have a computer, and Jane's Facebook updates were mostly photographs of her with friends in upscale bars. It was only by talking to them directly that I could find out how their lives were going.

I didn't text or tweet.

I have to admit there have been a few Monday nights when I was relieved to reach Jason's answering machine instead of Jason himself. He was always desperate for money, more money than I could give him. Since he had dropped out of Pratt Institute and moved to Santa Fe, his quest for the meaning of life hadn't taught him the secret of how to attract cash. He could expect no financial help from Colin, who was still furious with him.

"He won't find the meaning of life working in a tortilla factory," Colin fumed. "That's what college is for."

This was no doubt true, but unlike his sisters, Jason had never cracked the secret of succeeding in school either. He had asked incisive questions in class, but by the time the answer came he was thinking about something else.

Tonight though there was a lot of "Mom, guess what!?"

"I've got a job building an adobe house." (Jason.)

"You won't believe who I met at this sports club!" (Jane.)

"Dr. Jonas thinks I've got a good chance of getting into the vet school." (Hannah.)

Because I had been so young when the children were born or maybe because there had been so many so soon, I had never worked out what they should be when they grew up. I wanted them to be good people and happy with their lives, but I had no blueprints for them. On the other hand, maybe I hadn't needed to decide their life paths. Colin had plans for all of us.

Buoyed by their successes tonight, I stayed up filling book orders until way past midnight.

TUESDAY MORNING I stopped at Qwikjava and bought an insulated cup and a chicken wrap. As intriguing as the Eriksons were, I wasn't planning to eat with them every day.

The room was still stuffy when I unlocked the padlock and stepped inside, and I almost left the door open to air the studio out. But what if Eve Erikson decided to go for a stroll around the property, and found the door ajar? It would be a quick end to my book assessing career. I shut myself in once more.

Today the studio felt like less of a shrine. I was anxious to get to the books illustrated by Nate Erikson's forerunners, N. C. Wyeth, Rockwell Kent, and Howard Pyle, and see if any had been signed. But that was like eating dessert first. I made myself go upstairs and bring down the *Complete Sherlock Holmes* set that Nate had illustrated.

Considering that Conan Doyle's stories were dominated by the same two men, Nate's illustrations were as dramatic and varied as I had hoped. I especially admired the shadow of the ape outside the window terrifying the young woman in her bed, and the lurid settings of the opium dens. What an imagination Nate had had! When I checked the valuation, I discovered that, as a complete set, the Holmes books were worth several thousand dollars.

Still, it became tedious examining identical books in German, Swedish, Japanese, and a dozen other languages, checking each one for variations. By noon I was sick of the hound who hadn't bothered to bark in the night.

And then I came across a five-by-seven photograph, stuck in a copy of *Der Hund von Baskerville*. The picture showed the same fair-haired man as in the portrait in the dining room, but older, his smile nuanced. He was holding on to a squirming child of three or four with tangled dark hair who I assumed was Morgan. Restraining her, actually. She was pulling away, half off his lap, looking as if she were impatient to jump down and make someone's life miserable.

An interesting photo, though not one you would frame. I stared at it, considering what I should do with it. If I returned it to *Der Hund von Baskerville*, the photo ran the risk of being undiscovered if the books were ever sold. I had a collection of things left behind in the books I bought, from dental appointment reminders to ticket stubs and love letters. This ephemera was probably worthless, but I couldn't bring myself to discard this evidence of once-lived lives.

The only items I did discard were reviews that people had tucked inside books, a major bookseller annoyance. Cheap newsprint turned brown and stained the inside covers. Taped-in reviews left a yellow bruise where the tape had worn away. I was happy not to find any of these in Nate's books.

I looked at the photo of Nate and Morgan again. It felt presumptuous to prop it up on the studio table. Instead I left it lying flat.

CHAPTER NINE

I WAS ABOUT to get out my chicken wrap—I usually eat and work at the same time —when there was a knock on the door and Bianca came in. "Lunchtime," she said warmly. "Everyone was so happy to meet you yesterday. They were saying at breakfast how interesting you are."

Really? Nate Erikson's family found me interesting? I tried to remember what we had talked about. I knew I couldn't skip lunch with them after that. Still, tomorrow I would leave the grounds well before 1 p.m. There was no reason to wear out my welcome.

Mama wasn't at the table. As we were sitting down, her aide, whom Claude called Bessie, stepped into the dining room to say that Miss Eve was feeling poorly and would have a tray in her room.

There was still the family toast to the patriarch, but with a sense of giddiness, as if the teacher had stepped out of the room. Only Rosa stared wide-eyed at the flow-ered urn as if imagining her father inside.

"Are you coming to the show Saturday night?" Puck asked me, as he spooned homemade applesauce onto his plate.

"What show?"

"What show?" He raised his eyebrows at his sister. "Shame on you, Bianca."

I could feel her bristle. "I assumed she knew about it. Anyway," she explained to me, "Guild Hall is honoring the family and our contribution to the East End in a me-morial to Dad. There's an exhibition of Dad's and Regan's paintings, and a concert of Puck's music Saturday night. That's by invitation only, of course. But starting Monday, the paintings will be open to the public."

"But I want Delhi at the *concert*," Puck said. "Hon-estly, Bianca, you're thick as a board sometimes. Why not have someone there who actually looks like an artist, who isn't *just* eye candy. There'll be enough of that and I still have a few tickets left for friends." He winked at me. "Truth is, most of my friends wouldn't be caught dead in black tie."

"I'd love to come." I smiled back. I didn't know if he was calling me eye candy or not, but at least he'd remem-bered my name.

Bianca rallied. "Puck, you'll need to give her two tick-ets. So she can bring Colin Fitzhugh."

What was she talking about? I didn't mind bringing a guest—but Colin? We hadn't been out together in ages. Inviting him would make him think I was trying to lure him back. *He* had left *me*. It wasn't that there was tension between us, we just knew how to make each other crazy. After four children and twenty-five years, we had become experts.

"Who's Regan?" I asked, to forestall making a commitment about Colin.

"You don't know who Regan is either?" Puck feigned surprise. "Bianca didn't tell you about the prodigal daughter?"

"Oh, knock it off, Puck." Bianca's cheeks glowed red. "It's no big mystery. Regan lives upstate in Columbia County. She's an artist, that's all."

"I don't know why they included her in the show," Claude complained. "Her work is nowhere near as good as Dad's."

"She's an Erikson. And she's gotten good press and sales."

"At least she's not staying at the house," Lynn said as if to pacify her husband.

I was dying to know why everyone hated her.

GRETCHEN SERVED A homemade blueberry cobbler and ice cream, of which Puck and Rosa had seconds, then we pushed back our chairs to leave.

Rosa, who had been silent for the meal, suddenly said to me, "I'm an artist too."

"Really?"

"Would you like to see?" Today she was wearing a loose-fitting blue shirt the same color as Nate Erikson's smock in the painting.

"Sure."

"No, you don't." Claude looked up from checking the pens in his pocket. "She paints on *china*."

"That's okay."

Wrong answer. He angrily jammed his chair into the table, and bent his head to whisper something to Lynn. She nodded gravely and gave me a quick look.

Was Rosa that bad an artist? Even if her painting on china was a sentimental horror, her amateurism hardly tarnished the reputation of the Erikson family.

Lynn joined us on the side of the house. "Can I come too?" she asked Rosa in her let's-be-friends way.

"No! You're not invited." Rosa grabbed my arm as if we were in the middle of a kindergarten brawl and pulled me down the hill toward the second white chalet.

I looked back and saw Lynn watching, but she didn't try to follow us.

As we got closer to Rosa's chalet, I saw that the lawn was filled with outdoor furniture and rusted barbecues. A squadron of chipped dwarfs and a skunk protected Snow White. It was my worst nightmare of a yard sale, the kind I would drive past before anything could catch my eye. The books at such sales were rarely worth it.

I inched my way up the porch steps sideways, between flower urns. Rosa pushed the door back as far as she could. "Do you think things have feelings?"

"You mean like, if you put a chair out in the trash, it would feel rejected?" I asked.

"Yes! You wouldn't believe the things I've had to rescue." Suddenly her words were spilling out, as if she had found an ally. "Look at this." She touched the back of her hand to a carved wooden étagère crammed with porcelain miniatures. Since the shelves were mirrored behind, the effect was dizzying. "Someone was *giving* this away on Craigslist. They wouldn't even take money for it."

I noticed that a few of the carved pieces were missing and the mirror in back was cracked in several places.

At the end of the hall was the kitchen, which she had turned into an art studio. Dozens of delicate bottles were lined up in color order, and stacks of white plates had a table all to themselves. The table blocked the back door. I could smell turpentine and other solvents, and noticed a kiln on the counter beside the stove. Whatever she made, she was serious about her work. The pressure to be creative in this family had to be enormous and even if Rosa painted the usual things on plates, flowers and Christmas decorations, I gave her credit for trying.

"I do the master design and the manufacturer copies it. Unless I'm selling it by itself as an original to a gallery."

Can't blame her for dreaming.

"This is my latest series." Her voice was shy. "It's called 'Feeding the Hungry.'"

Touching my arm as lightly as a whisper, she brought me to the back of the kitchen to where a series of dinner plates were displayed on a harvest table. But instead of cornucopias of fruits and vegetables, this was another kind of raw food. Even though they were black images on a white background, there was something too real about the hamburger meat twisted into brains and the bumpy skin on chicken breasts. The meats were accompanied by potatoes still in their jackets, and uncooked broccoli and asparagus stalks.

I was floored. Where did this originality and humor come from? "These are wonderful! How long have you been making them?"

"A long time. I won a prize for 'Trash.'" She reached for a large black album on another table.

I hoped I wouldn't be looking at maggots and gnawed bones, but these designs showed crumpled Doritos bags and crushed soda cans turned into art. A stack of batteries formed an Egyptian pyramid. At first I wasn't sure what I was looking at, then laughed out loud.

Rosa's open face beamed. "I knew you'd get it. Galleries always want more of these than I can make."

"I can see why. I'd love a set. Do you work as Rosa Erikson?"

Her mouth twisted. "I'd never use *Erikson*."

She didn't tell me what name she did use as she led me back to the front door.

CHAPTER TEN

As IMPRESSED AS I was by Rosa's plates, I was happy to be out of her cottage. It was too claustrophobic, too intense. The clutter reminded me of the times I had to go with my mother on visits to ancient parishioners and sit in dust-filled parlors where yellowed antimacassars gave the rooms their only color. Rosa also gave me the feeling I had had as that child of having to choose my words carefully to not give offense.

I took in a deep breath of salt air. Rosa's accumulation was not on the scale of the Collier brothers yet, but if there was ever a fire . . .

Bianca was waiting for me on her porch, motionless in a yellow rocker.

"So you survived Rosa's clutter." She said it flatly, as if I had defied her by going down there.

"Her work is amazing. Why didn't Claude want me to see it?"

"It was her environment he didn't want you to see."
Then she reconsidered. "No, it was both. It galls him that
someone that ditzy can make so much money and he can't."

"You think she's ditzy?" Unusual certainly, maybe
bordering on idiot savant, but "ditzy" seemed a mean-
spirited label.

"Let's just say she's one of a kind."

"Aren't we all." I wondered why Bianca seemed so
hard on her sister. "Did she always have so much stuff?"

"It's gotten worse. The mess drove my father crazy. He
loved her work, he was the one who introduced her to
the galleries, but hated the way she lived . . . In fact—"
She broke off and slid her eyes in the direction of Rosa's
cottage, as if deciding how much she should share with
me. "Right before he died, he gave her an ultimatum.
Either she clean up the cottage, get rid of everything, or
she would have to leave. He even threatened to have her
committed."

"To a mental hospital? How could he do that?"

"He was Nate Erikson."

"But still."

"Delhi, he wouldn't have really done it." She looked
amused. "It was only a threat, to try and get her to act
normal. I don't know why he cared so much."

I leaned against one of the porch posts. "He was her
father."

Instead of answering, Bianca stood up to walk me back
to the studio. When we were nearly to the door, she said,
"Rosa's real father was our groundskeeper and driver. He
and his wife did the grocery shopping, and she was our

cook. But then they were hit by a train. Rosa was in the backseat, she was only five. There were no gates or warning lights out here back then, trains never came this far out."

The image of a screeching metal collision, a car tossed and crumpled, bleeding bodies and terror spread across my mind, and I couldn't wish it away. "How *terrible*. Is that where she got the scar?"

"I guess. I was only three, I didn't really understand. Rosa was in the hospital a long time with a head injury and lacerations and when she came out, my parents adopted her. But people can tell she isn't one of us."

I hadn't been sure. When she'd said she didn't use the name Erikson, I'd assumed she didn't want to be confused with Nate or Regan. If Nate had been threatening to evict her or have her committed . . . or worse, been trying to make her discard items that were emotionally dependent on her for their survival . . . had it come down to a choice between them—or him?

As I DROVE home, I cast about for someone besides Colin I could take to the concert. The thought of my bookseller friends made me laugh. Marty would show up in his red Cadillac T-shirt, Susie Pevney in her Mets baseball gear. For a fleeting moment I considered Colin's colleague, Bruce Adair, a critical presence in the poetry world. Bianca would be happy enough with Bruce. But in our latest encounters, he had started propositioning me, and I didn't want to give him any hope. No, I would have to ask Colin. He even had a tux.

When I got home and checked my messages, I saw Marty had called wanting to know what I had decided to do about the Old Frigate, a message I ignored. Instead I dialed Colin's cell phone.

Four rings, then "Hey-lo."

"Hi, it's me. Do you want to go to a benefit concert at Guild Hall Saturday night? It's formal, but I have two tickets. It's honoring the Eriksons."

"Delhi, what are you talking about?"

I slowed down and explained.

"Of course I'll go," he said when I finished talking. He made it sound as if he were doing me a favor, like going to a wake or picking someone up at the train station.

"In a tux."

"I get that. The question is, what are you wearing?"

"Oh, I'll find something."

"Delhi, do me a favor. At least go to a department store."

"Um."

"No thrift shop getup! Promise me."

"Not even a tiara?"

"*Delhi.*"

"Okay, okay."

"We'll eat out first," he decided. "We need to talk."

We need to talk. The words I least liked to hear, no matter who was saying them to me. Coming from a husband, you knew the conversation would not be how to best celebrate Valentine's Day.

On the other hand, the food would probably be good.

CHAPTER ELEVEN

WHEN I OPENED the studio door on Wednesday morning, I smelled burnt paper.

Not the books! Dear God, not the books!

Without putting down my coffee or computer case, I rushed to the center of the room and looked around. It seemed exactly as I'd left it, down to the pad I used for notes still open on the table. Gradually I realized the smell seemed stronger in the direction of the fireplace. But why would someone have made a fire? Last night had been a typical September evening, brisk, but not cool enough to need any heat. Summer clung frantically to Long Island like an aging crone, unable to admit her heyday had passed, until one morning the trees were all vivid oranges and golds and rimmed by frost.

But that day was far away.

Puzzled, I moved over to the hearth and looked in. A blackened page curled like a cringing hand on top of the bed of ancient ashes. I didn't need the glossy white corner and darkened faces to tell me it was the photograph of Morgan and Nate that had been on the worktable. I touched the edge with one finger and the darkness it gave off coated my throat and nostrils.

My God. Someone had come in, seen the photo, and struck a match to the edge. They had deliberately set fire to the photograph of Nate and his squirming granddaughter and left the evidence in plain view. *Wicked.* That is what my parents would have called it and for once I agreed with them. Who could be so cruel? The smoky air made my eyes tear and I stumbled back to the worktable. The destruction made me even more certain that the drownings had been no accident.

Shaken, I sat down in the metal chair and scrolled through my e-mail messages without reading them. Finally I stood up.

I needed to breathe. Nobody had told me I couldn't walk around the grounds. I padlocked the door and set off.

That was how I found the pool.

I had just passed Rosa's chalet on my right when I noticed a rectangular group of cedars. The shrubs were the upright variety planted as windbreaks. As I drew closer, I saw that a gap had been left and the pool just beyond. All along I had been picturing the pool out in the open, centrally located in front of the cottages. But it had been hidden here.

The cedars were tall, over my head. I walked through the opening and stared down. The pool must have been emptied after it happened but it wasn't empty now. A foot of water had collected in the deep end, water so dirty and unappealing that I didn't want to get any closer. Friezes of mermaids and water sprites had been painted on the sides of the pool. When I reached the center I looked back and saw Triton—or was it Neptune?— blowing his horn at the deep end. Under my feet the blue-and-white pattern of tiles was grimy.

I realized something else. No one would have been able to see what was happening in the pool from outside.

"Don't jump," a voice begged me, and I whirled around. Aunt Gretchen was standing on the tier of ground above me, looking down.

"Don't worry, I forgot my towel," I called back, then climbed a set of stone steps to reach her.

She was taller than I had realized, wearing dirt-stained jeans and a red windbreaker, a navy calico bandana covering her bright hair. She had the boniness of someone who had been fleshy but lost weight. Behind her was a lush, end-of-season garden planted in perfect rows. Crimson balls of tomatoes hung heavily against dark leaves, and I spotted more of the beans we had eaten the day before. Pumpkin and melon vines snaked over the ground like connecting cords. The garden was protected by a high fence and netting.

"What a gorgeous garden. Do you do it yourself?"

"Every last leaf. We had a gardener once, but he—" She stopped then, as if that story had an unhappy ending. "By the way, I'm Gretchen Erikson, Nate's cousin. He grew up with my family." She put out a weathered hand and smiled at me. "Aunt Gretchen to everyone else."

"You're his cousin? But—you do all the cooking!"

She laughed. "It keeps me busy. There's nothing worse than an idle old lady."

I was about to protest that she wasn't that old when I heard a scraping on the steps behind me and turned around.

"What's going on here?" Bianca sounded tense. To get here so quickly she would have had to have been following me.

"Your friend was admiring my garden," Gretchen said. "I can't think why, when it's such a fright. They'll be bringing me the straw to mulch it next week." She sighed. "Sometimes I wonder why I bother."

"Because you love to see everything grow."

"I do. But it's not the same without Nate."

"Nothing is." Bianca poked at an errant root with her toe.

"And my precious angel. I can't believe she's not here either, jumping up and down to see how big the pumpkins are getting."

"*Don't.*"

"I never realized how blessed we were. You expect it will go on forever." Then Gretchen seemed to pull herself together. "Maybe once the garden's bedded down, I'll do some traveling. It's been too long since I've been to Italy."

"But we'll starve to death!"

"Oh, you'll manage. What will you do when I can no longer cook at all?"

"Put you on an ice floe, I guess." Then Bianca gave my back a jab. "Come on. You have work to do."

"Ow!" I reached around and rubbed the spot. I followed her with ill grace down the stone steps.

"What *will* you do when she can't cook anymore?"

Bianca's pale eyes widened and she gave me a scornful smirk. "Starve to death, probably."

I laughed. It had been a silly question.

"I can't imagine Gretchen not being around. She took care of us when we were little, while my parents were working."

"Your parents worked?" I couldn't imagine it. That would be like Queen Elizabeth helping out at her local deli.

"Not at jobs. Mama painted watercolors, mostly flowers, and you know what my father did. We'd have lunch, the way we still do, then my father would play classical music and read to us. After that we'd sit around the table drawing or painting. *Life* magazine came and took pictures of us when I was seven."

"Who was the best artist?"

"Not me! Rosa was good at making things look realistic." We were passing her cottage and Bianca gave a censorious look at the clutter. "Regan only wanted to draw fairies and princesses, and Claude drew a lot of battle scenes with stick figures. They were awful."

"What about Puck?"

"I'd like to say he was awful too, but he wasn't. He inherited the family gift and my parents pinned their hopes on him to carry on the family tradition. The trouble was, his passion was music but he didn't get any encouragement." She laughed. "What's the opposite of encouragement? Since my father died, he hasn't picked up a brush.

The concert Saturday night is his first public appearance. He's nervous as a goat in a kid glove factory."

I laughed.

"One of my father's pet expressions. Pardon the pun."

By my calculations, Puck was in his early thirties. How excruciating had the pressure been to set aside his dreams and become another Nate? Excruciating enough for him to end the situation and save his own life?

I shook away that thought. First Rosa and now Puck. Since I had decided that Nate and Morgan's deaths were not accidental, I had been fitting people out for prison garb. There was nothing to suggest that a family member had been involved.

Then I remembered the burnt photograph in the fireplace.

CHAPTER TWELVE

I MADE SURE that I left the studio by twelve-thirty so I wouldn't have to have lunch with the family. I was out of sorts and wanted to be alone. There was no way I could still be feeling Bianca's poke in my back except metaphorically, but the more I thought about it, the more outrageous it seemed. Giving a friend a playful prod was one thing—but Bianca and I weren't yet friends. If we would ever be. Maybe she had meant to be teasing, maybe Gretchen's comment about Morgan had upset her, but coming from an employer it was out of line.

I picked up my bag while enumerating her offenses: She had decided I was her "collaborator" without even asking me. She hadn't thought I was good enough to be invited to Puck's concert. She—

Oh, come on. She just lost her father and her only child. Cut her some slack.

Fair enough. But I still wanted to have lunch on my own.

I made a clean getaway Wednesday. Thursday I was nearly to my van when Lynn, Claude's wife, climbed out of a dark green Toyota. "Am I late?" she asked breathlessly. "I got held up at the shelter. Are you going in to lunch?"

"No, I have some errands. What shelter?"

"A Safe Haven. It's for victims of domestic violence and their children. My job is to get the women happily settled into new homes with all the furnishings they need. I'm sorry you won't be at lunch. We missed you yesterday too."

"I know. Gretchen's a good cook."

"I was so afraid she wouldn't stay on."

"You mean after Nate?"

"There was so much bad feeling after it happened. Gretchen and Morgan had gone for a walk in the back woods, but Morgan ran ahead to the house and Gretchen couldn't keep up with her. When she didn't see Morgan, she didn't think to look in the pool. Claude and Puck felt that if she had, or if she had kept Morgan under control, none of this would have happened."

"Where was Bianca?"

Lynn's face turned blank as an unprimed canvas. "I'm not sure. She was used to having Morgan's au pair take care of her in the mornings, but that day she wasn't— Anyway, it doesn't matter. All I know is, when my son was little, *I* was the one who took care of him and got him ready for school."

"I thought Eriksons didn't go to school."

She rolled her eyes. "Peter did. I threatened to take him and leave, otherwise, I'd seen what growing up wild did to the others. Nate and Eve finally agreed he could go to Hampton Day School. Now he's at Deerfield."

"Why were they so against education?"

"The usual reasons. They felt that rote learning stifled creativity and that they could do a better job. *I* think it was a mistake. They didn't do my husband any favors." She gave an anxious glance at the house. "I'd better go wash up. Sure you won't stay?"

"Maybe tomorrow." I opened the van door thoughtfully. No one had mentioned an au pair.

An Illustrated Death

CHAPTER THIRTEEN

ON FRIDAY MORNING, I decided to take a break from Nate Erikson's work and catalog the illustrators that had been his inspiration. I felt like Howard Carter exploring King Tut's tomb, the treasures were that amazing. *Howard Pyle's Book of Pirates. The Yearling* by N. C. Wyeth, a first edition *Moby Dick* by Rockwell Kent. I lingered long over the work of Maxfield Parrish. These artists were dead now, and the tradition of beautifully illustrated classics was dying too. What effect would that have had on Nate Erikson's career?

It was not even noon when Bianca knocked and stepped inside. "We missed you the past couple of days."

"I had errands," I apologized insincerely.

"That's understandable. But we'll see you today? We want to talk about the memorial tomorrow night.""

"Sure. Thanks."

OVER CHICKEN MARSALA, the family speculated about who would be attending the memorial.

"I don't know why they didn't have it in August, when more people were out here," Claude complained. "The season is almost over."

"Sweetie, your family's not the Kennedys. It's on a Saturday night, after all."

Lynn's comment earned her a scowl from Mama. "We may not have been the Kennedys, but we founded Springs!"

"Well, Krasner and Pollock were already here," Claude conceded.

"*Them.*"

"I suggested doing something at Guild Hall because I wanted to honor Dad's memory. His legacy. But this feels like it's turning into a circus." Bianca frowned at her lunch as if it were somehow to blame. "Everything's always about *him* anyway. No one remembers that my little girl died too."

"Oh, we remember." Claude's knife slid off the chicken breast and screeched onto the plate. "How could we forget when she caused it all?"

"You don't know that! You weren't there. Anything could have happened. Maybe she saw that Dad was in trouble and tried to pull him out."

A harsh laugh from Puck. He raised his eyes to heaven. "Morgan as lifeguard? That's a new one. That brat wouldn't have saved an ant crossing her path. If you hadn't brought her into this family . . ."

Bianca gasped and Lynn dropped her knife. "That's *enough*." Lynn turned on Puck. "What's wrong with you? She was an innocent little child."

"Not so innocent that—"

"Enough!" Claude echoed his wife. "Puck, you're way out of line."

"Don't tell me you don't feel the same way."

Mama watched the fireworks complacently.

Rosa stared down at her plate.

Were they really talking about a four-year-old child they had all been related to? How mean did you have to be to call a dead child a brat? At least Lynn and Claude had protested. But what kind of grandmother sat there as if listening to a discussion of a neighbor's unruly dog? If Lynn hadn't spoken up, I would have had to.

I turned my head to look at Bianca, who was fighting to not cry. I reached out and put my hand over hers, pressing hard.

Puck put down his fork and sighed. "Sorry, Bee. It was just a stupid joke."

"Never mind," she said finally.

"It's this damn memorial that has everyone on edge. I don't—"

His apology was interrupted by a smart rapping at the front door.

Claude jumped up. "I think it's for me."

"Psychic now?" Puck raised his eyebrows.

"He's expecting something from Japan," Lynn explained to the table.

After three or four minutes Claude returned with a

scowl, carrying a hanger draped in clear plastic with a dry cleaner's logo. It looked like a woman's jacket made of nubby, olive green silk.

Gretchen came in behind him. "That's mine."

"Why, it's your Saks Fifth Avenue suit," said Eve, bemused. "Imagine."

"I took it in to be cleaned for the memorial."

"Does it still fit?" Bianca asked.

"I hope so. I may have an important announcement to make, something I know Nate would have wanted."

"Don't tell me," Puck said. "You're expecting."

No one laughed.

"Well, don't keep us in suspense," Lynn smiled at her.

"I have one more thing to check out tomorrow."

Eve pushed back her chair, signaling that lunch was over.

I wanted to catch up with Bianca, but going down the front steps Puck said into my ear, "This family is so screwed up."

He was the last person I wanted to talk to, but I stopped. "I thought this was supposed to be like the Garden of Eden."

"That's what they wanted us to think. I know you think I'm terrible, but you know what they used to call me? 'The Accident.' Because I was the youngest. If it hadn't been for my parents, they would have drowned me too."

Drowned you too?

I started to ask him what he meant, but he winked and turned in the opposite direction.

AT BIANCA'S CHALET, I called to her through the screen door.

"Delhi? It's open."

It was the first time I had actually been inside the cottage. Compared to Rosa's identically shaped living room, the space was calm and harmonious. The predominant colors were daffodil yellow and leaf green, and the tiny tables held interesting objects—small framed photographs, a china cat in a calico design, miniature enameled boxes.

On a smaller chair sat a teddy bear with a red bow around its neck, waiting for someone who would never hug it again. Its innocence broke my heart.

Bianca was sitting on a puffy quilted sofa with a yellow flower design, a photo album in her lap.

"Are you okay?" I asked.

She gave me a bleak look, her eyes a map of red lines. "That's the definition of insanity, isn't it—doing the same thing over and over and expecting different results? They never cared about Morgan. Gretchen was the only one."

"But why?"

"Because she wasn't really an Erikson. Isn't that silly? I had five miscarriages before we adopted her, so I thought they'd be happy for me. Hah. Puck's right about one thing though. Morgan was a hard case."

"Morgan was adopted?" I didn't want that to change my perception of the tragedy, but something inside me eased a little. I hadn't understood what Puck meant when he accused Bianca of bringing Morgan into the family. I'd thought he meant it metaphorically.

Bianca leaned back on the couch and closed her eyes. "When we finally brought her home from Romania, she was almost two. It was too late, she'd been too neglected. She'd have these tantrums sometimes and bite anyone who tried to get near her. She had to be supervised constantly. I even had an au pair so I could get some sleep."

She reached back to the table behind her and handed me a small framed photograph of a dark-haired child. "She was the most beautiful child you'd ever seen. I finally knew what it felt like to love someone more than anything. And she loved *me*. When we saw her in the orphanage I opened up my arms and she ran right into them. I didn't believe them when they said it was a bad sign."

"Why was it bad?"

"They called it an affective disorder. She'd go to anyone at all. But she was so alive and loving and hopeful, she didn't understand when people got angry with her." That brought fresh tears.

"Look." She stood up and motioned me to follow.

We went into the hall to a room filled with shelves of stuffed animals. A large castle stood in one corner with a princess figurine on the balcony. Bianca opened the closet and showed me a long row of little dresses, princess costumes, and a dozen pairs of shoes on a white wooden rack below. She closed the door again. "Sometimes I just come in here and cry. I don't know what to do with anything."

"It's only been three months. It's too soon." I could barely speak myself.

"I had so many plans for her."

Back in the living room we sat side by side on the couch. "I try to tell myself that it was better for her this way. I think about the years ahead, when I would have had to try and find a place for her in the world. I was worried what she might do to other children and all the rejection she would feel. And yet . . . I don't believe it."

We sat in silence, Bianca staring at the pink album she was holding again. "You know what the very worst thing was? I don't know if I can even tell you without . . ."

"Go ahead and cry."

"When Gretchen came to find me after it happened and we got to the pool, Rosa was wailing and the others were all kneeling around Dad trying to give him CPR. I couldn't even see Morgan at first. Then I saw she was lying so still on the cement all by herself. Like a doll someone had forgotten to bring in. It was the end of her life and no one cared!"

In the next minute I was hugging Bianca, holding her while she sobbed and sobbed.

I felt something long-frozen start to thaw in me as well and then I was crying hard too.

Caitlin, Caitlin, Caitlin.

CHAPTER FOURTEEN

AFTER LEAVING BIANCA'S cottage it was hard to go back to the studio. The pleasures of that morning seemed far away, replaced by the sadness that was real life. I had things of my own I wanted to think about. I reminded myself that I would have all weekend to visit the past, but that now I had to finish assessing the books I had pulled out and tidy up the studio.

It was nearly six when I zipped away my laptop and looked around to make sure nothing was out of place. I left the burnt photograph in the fireplace.

Once I was out on Cooper's Farm Lane the sun was nowhere in evidence and dusk had started to creep in. Automatically I switched on my headlights in the gloom, then realized that another car had pulled behind me from the side of the road, its bright lights flooding my mirrors like a rude gesture.

It seemed an odd coincidence that another car would

be right in back of me on this deserted country lane. When Jackson Pollock raced down these roads in his convertible, killing himself and a young woman passenger, it was hours before anyone came by and discovered the carnage.

The mystery car hugged my fender like a magazine salesman. Blinded by its glaring lights, all I could tell was that it was a large, late-model black sedan. When I reached the sign at Sagabonac Road, I was too nervous to come to a full stop and kept going, thankful that there was no traffic from the cross street. It didn't help that I felt wrung out emotionally from my afternoon with Bianca, facing once again how dark the world could be.

The car started beeping its horn rhythmically like an audience clapping for a matinee to start.

Drivers will beep at you sometimes to point out that you have a flat tire. But other times it's a ploy to make you stop. On the highway to Pompeii from Rome one summer afternoon, three men in a battered green Fiat pulled up beside us and began honking and gesturing frantically. Colin glanced at them, then pressed the door lock button and drove faster. Our pursuers kept up the charade for several miles before falling away.

Think, Delhi.

I could pull into a driveway and try to get to a house. But the other car would be right behind me and by the time I got out of the van, I could easily be grabbed or shot. *Call the police*—except that my phone was in my bag on the floor and I'd have to stop the van to reach it. I'd heard that you should drive to the nearest police precinct and honk your horn outside, but I wasn't familiar enough with this part of the island to know where that was.

The other car stopped honking, but kept following closely.

At Montauk Highway, I had to stop for a red light. As soon as I did, the driver of the other car jumped out, came over, and rapped on my van window.

It was Charles Tremaine, the bookseller from Amagansett. And Manhattan.

I rolled the window down. "My God, I thought you were a carjacker! Or a rapist."

"This is the Hamptons, sweetheart. And, nothing personal, but why would anyone want to steal this?" He gestured at my 1999 van.

His tone was surprisingly unfriendly, but I laughed. "It's doubtful. And I'm even older."

"We need to talk. Flaherty's is down the road on the right."

FLAHERTY'S IS ONE of those East End taverns covered in white clapboard that looks more like a house than a bar. It was the folding sign with a Heineken medallion next to the front door advertising "Happy Hour!" that made me pull into the driveway. As I parked and walked past the sign, I saw that it was advertising "Raw Clams," and "Lobster Rolls with Fries," in loopy red letters.

I waited for Charles Tremaine to get out of his car and meet me at the door. He looked like a true Hamptonite, dressed in gray slacks, a pale blue V-neck cardigan and expensive loafers. His silvery hair was in perfect order. How long had he been waiting on the road for me to leave? We crossed the threshold into a room that smelled of beer and lemon freshener. To my right was a narrow bar, the stools crammed with people. To the left were small wooden tables with red-and-white checked cloths beneath mirrors advertising liquors.

Charles managed to find us a tiny table in the back corner but didn't sit down. Instead he turned toward the bar, then, as an afterthought, asked, "Do you want anything?"

So this wasn't a date. "Chardonnay." *And you can pay for it yourself for frightening me.*

The empty table next to ours had a small black bowl of pretzels. I reached over and set it in front of me.

Charles brought back what appeared to be a double scotch for himself and set my wine down without looking at me.

"Thanks." I picked up the glass and tilted it slightly toward him. "To the end of a perfect work week."

He snorted. "For years, my colleagues and I have been dying to get our hands on the Erikson library. I've made my wishes clear to the family. I knew Nate personally. When I asked about it last Saturday, I was told Eve would never allow it. Now I turn around and some . . ." He didn't know what to call me that wouldn't make me get up and walk out of the bar, so he let the characterization hang in the air.

"How do you know what I'm doing there?"

"They didn't hire you to wash the floors."

"I thought you worked in Manhattan."

He glared at me. "I have an assistant. And I'll tell you frankly, I can't believe Eve is allowing it. Does she even know if you're qualified? What are your qualifications anyway?"

We were on dangerous ground. I took a long sip of my wine. "Have you seen Eve lately?"

"No," he admitted. "She hasn't been out since he passed. And they were big partygoers. They gave parties too, for Midsummer's Night or a croquet marathon. But he was the one with the zest for life. That's what makes his death so ironic."

"Do people think what happened was an accident?"

He looked at me and I saw that his eyes were a true gray, the color of suede gloves men sometimes wore with formal attire. "What else would it be? He'd be the last person to commit suicide. Not that he had an easy life, he lost his father in the war and his mother to breast cancer. He was raised by Gretchen's parents."

"Is that why he didn't go to college?"

"He didn't go to college?" Charles worked on his drink. "I didn't know that. His uncle was a well-known Shakespeare scholar at Brown. Somebody told me they never got along though."

"What's Eve's background?"

He laughed. "Eve the Southern debutante? Charleston plantation, horseback riding, coming-out parties. Nate wasn't what her family raised her for. He showed them though. Anyway, let's talk about *you*."

"All I'm doing is appraising the books. I'm not buying

them, I can't. From what Bianca told me, they'll probably go to auction."

Ethically I couldn't put a price on a book and then offer to buy it. My only chance to own any was to bid for them along with everyone else.

"It's a shame to break up the collection. Tell me what's there exactly."

I smiled. "You know I can't do that." He couldn't really be expecting me to betray client confidentiality. But what if he went to Eve Erikson, presuming on old friendship, and made her an offer to buy the books outright? She would become hysterical if she learned that someone had been in her husband's studio touching them.

"Look." I took another sip of wine, playing for time. "I'll keep you posted on what's happening. I'll let you know when I finish, and what the family has decided to do. Once I'm done I can tell you more about the books. You were right, there are some wonderful association copies. I promise to keep you in the loop."

He gave me a dry look. "Don't do me any favors. But I can see why they'd want an outsider for the appraisal. I just don't get why they'd pick you. To think, if I hadn't changed your number . . ." He turned his wrist to see his Rolex. "I've got to go. My wife will think I'm having an affair."

"Perish the thought."

He winked and stood up. "You don't know my wife. We'll be in touch."

I had no doubt that we would.

CHAPTER FIFTEEN

I WAS RUNNING out of time to buy a dress for the memorial. Resisting the siren call of just one more sale—a sale that might have the book I'd been looking for all my life—I made myself drive over to Veterans' Thrift on Jericho Turnpike. The store was cavernous, a converted airplane hangar which displayed long, jumbled racks of clothing and dry goods. I bought most of my sweatshirts here. The rack labeled "Formals" was nearly too packed to sort through, but I pushed through it. Unless I wanted to look like a 1970s prom queen or the grandmother of the bride, there was little to choose from.

I continued on to Goodwill a mile farther down the road, and there I stumbled on a royal blue velvet dress. It wasn't floor-length, it ended at my knees, but it had a full skirt and an iridescent blue-green satin flower pinned to the waist. It fit perfectly and gave my eyes some color. I could add matching eye shadow and wear my hair up. No doubt it would have been more practical to buy something in black, but for $11.99 I decided I could splurge.

COLIN LOOKED ME over carefully when I opened the door Saturday night, a father long practiced in sending his daughters back upstairs to change.

"Very nice," he said finally, holding my arm to turn me and inspect my French twist. "Where's that gold chain I gave you?"

"Upstairs. You think I need jewelry?"

"Absolutely. And take off that Star Wars watch."

He had made reservations at Chez Marcelette in East Hampton, an intimate restaurant with designer food. Intimate also meant that the tables were as close as Kentucky cousins. Colin grimaced at the amount of room allotted to him, but managed to squeeze his generous body into a corner. No one looked surprised that he was wearing a tux.

When Jason was four, he had whispered to me, "Is Daddy Santa Claus?" That was even before Colin's thick beard had turned white.

I thought he'd been asking if Colin was responsible for his Christmas presents, and said, "No, of course not. Santa lives at the North Pole."

Jason had taken another look at Colin sitting in his wingback chair, his reading glasses perched on the tip of his round nose. "Well, is he his *brother*?"

Colin had gone on to cultivate the Santa Claus persona, showing a large and generous spirit to the people who worshipped him, especially archeology students and aspiring poets. And to his family, as long as he approved of what we were doing.

"How was Utah?" I asked, looking up from the menu. I had already decided on the lobster-stuffed ravioli with a truffle reduction, something I didn't often make at home.

"Too damn hot. We excavated some Anasazi dwellings, the usual kind. But I think I've had it with the Southwest."

"Really? Why?" I had loved traveling to that part of the world.

"Wait." He signaled the young waiter, who had already identified himself as Jeff, and ordered a bottle of vintage Côtes du Rhône. I was impressed.

I also knew not to ask him anything else until the wine was poured.

We were raising our glasses for the first momentous sip when he reached over to clink mine. "To new beginnings!"

Whose new beginnings? Ours? Had he brought me here to tell me he had found someone else? This was the man who had moved out of the farmhouse almost a year ago, blaming me because his life lacked zest. The one who reminded me that since I hadn't finished college, I was not fit to polish his commas.

"Salut!" he insisted.

"Salut," I echoed, trying to remember which country it was from.

"The truth is"—he lowered his eyes modestly—"they've offered me the chairmanship of the entire division."

"Wow. Congratulations. What does that mean exactly?"

A break as our waiter set down the house salad of walnuts, blue cheese, pears, and baby greens. I gave the salad a fond look. It cost as much as my dress had.

"More administrative decision making and less teaching, of course. More compensation, but they'll expect me to be around more. And I'll need to do more entertaining." He gave me a meaningful look.

I lowered the fork I had started to move toward my salad. Something about the way he was looking at me reminded me of Marty at the Old Frigate last week. While I had been happily trying to sell books, the men around me had been plotting an alternative universe.

He tilted his head and looked into a rosy future. "A man reaches a certain point where he is no longer willing to live life on the fly."

Another familiar ring. But this one was Jane Austen, declaring that a single man in possession of a fortune must be in need of a wife.

The trouble was, we had never had the fortune. Still, our life had been an adventure. I had been places I never would have gone. We'd always have Peru. And Berkeley. And Khartoum.

"It's time to buy a real house," he was saying, "a house that suits who I've become. One of those grand old Victorians in Stony Brook or a captain's home in Port Lewis. Somewhere we can give parties and hold receptions." He took a bite of salad. "I know you never cared much about fixing up the farmhouse. But something like this might inspire you."

He was right about the farmhouse. Although I'd turned the barn into my book retreat, I had treated the house itself as if it were a motel to which we returned whenever we were in town. We could have negotiated with the university to replace the harvest gold kitchen appliances that needed mercy killing, and gone to sales to buy tasteful antiques. But we hadn't. We were always off to another university for a guest lectureship, or sequestered at another archeological site. With three kids there were more pressing things to do when we were home.

"We can fix up the top floor for the grandchildren."

Considering that Jason and Hannah were too young to think about marriage and Jane had sworn off serious relationships, I decided he was in Santa Claus mode.

Jeff was back to clear our salad plates. I hadn't touched mine yet.

"Are you still working on that?"

"Slaving away," I assured him cheerfully.

Colin snorted. When a disappointed Jeff had gone, he said, "You could think about finishing your education and deciding what you want to do."

"I *am* doing something. It's called bookselling. What are your plans for my books anyway?"

"Your books? You mean the ones you sell? A lot of these houses have sheds out back."

"For eight thousand books?"

"You could scale down. Specialize in one area."

"I've thought of that," I admitted. What bookseller hasn't fantasized about concentrating on selling a few expensive books to wealthy collectors? I thought of Charles

Tremaine though I didn't know what he specialized in. But there were dealers on BookEm.com who looked down from that snowy summit at the rest of us selling ten-dollar books. The trick was to figure out how to scramble up there with them. Besides, I was fascinated by all the different kinds of books I sold. How could I turn my back on any of them?

"And you'd have to do something about your hippie wardrobe," he teased.

My wardrobe? *As if.*

Jeff was back. Without removing my untouched salad, he arranged a steaming bowl of pasta in front of me. "Pepper?"

"Yes, please."

He produced a pepper mill the size of a softball bat and twisted it over my plate.

Colin had ordered a large porterhouse steak with sweet potato fries, and was contentedly digging in.

"Remember the restaurant in Santa Fe where the waiters and waitresses suddenly went over to the piano and started singing songs from *The Music Man*?" I asked. We had turned and watched them, openmouthed. I couldn't imagine Jeff breaking into song.

"La Cantina. They still do. I was there this summer."

Without me. I was shocked at the depth of the wound that created. What adoring young graduate student had been there in my place? We had had a life, a good life together. If I had been more obliging . . . If he had stayed more intrigued by me . . .

I leaned forward, crushing the napkin in my lap. "Are you propositioning me?"

He laughed. "Can a man proposition his own wife?"

"I don't know. But you haven't said anything about love."

"*Love.*" He closed his eyes as if exposure to the brightness of the word might injure his corneas. Or perhaps it was to demonstrate that he was lost in thought. Finally he opened them and jabbed his fork at me. "Define love."

"Colin . . ." I paused for another bite of ravioli that melted to nothing in my mouth. "Don't do this to me. A year ago you decided that being married was holding you back. Living with me was keeping you out of the stratosphere where National Book Awards are given." *Shut up, Delhi. Be nice.* I tried again. "As you may remember, I was devastated. We'd been through a lot, but I never saw that coming. All of a sudden I was on my own and had to think about how to survive."

"You don't—"

I put up a hand to keep him quiet. "What I found out was, being by myself isn't that bad. It's not bad at all. I finally have a life I'm in control of. I can eat McDonald's every night if I want. So when you come along with what sounds more like a business proposition, I have a few questions."

The restaurant door slammed and the candle on our table flickered in agitation. "If you told me you loved me and planned to spend the rest of your life with me, that would be different."

Say it, Colin. Make it different.

He sighed and pushed back as far as he could in his chair—not very far. "What you don't understand is that life is a fast-flowing stream. You can't freeze relationships. We aren't where we were a year ago, and we don't know where we'll be in five years."

"That's the point. I have to know."

"Why do you need so many guarantees? Why can't you let things just play out? All I know is that I'm the new department head and that certain expectations come with the job. I can't go on living in a rented condo. What I'm offering you is a chance to be part of a great new adventure. A chance to trade in your Berkeley mentality for a truly adult life. We're not kids anymore."

"But without love." I saw that my hand was shaking and put my fork down quickly.

He stopped eating too. "Of course not without love. Loving you isn't the issue, you know that I do. All I'm asking is to see how things develop."

My face was burning. "I can't. Because if I give up the life I've made, I need to know that you won't decide in a year or two that you need fresh inspiration elsewhere."

"Then you'll be missing out on the most fantastic adventure we've ever had. You'll be consigning yourself to a lonely old age."

"Colin, I'm only forty-five! And they're *my* kids too."

"You're forgetting something: If we're not married, you can't stay on in the farmhouse and barn. It's university property."

Marty's proposition about running the Old Frigate crept into my mind. *No.* "You know what? That sounds a lot like blackmail."

He gave me his disappointed-professor glance. "That

is exactly the kind of fallacious thinking that you fall prey to. With more education—"

"Oh, don't lecture me; I'm not your ethnography class. You know why I dropped out of college. By the time we were settled in one place and the kids were older, I was more interested in other things. So just stop."

He raised his hands in surrender. "Okay, okay. It's just that you're so bright you could do whatever you want."

"I am doing whatever I want."

How did we get from buying a house together to getting a degree I didn't care about? Colin was the most infuriating man I'd ever known.

I had had enough ravioli and too much conversation. "We're going to be late."

CHAPTER SIXTEEN

GUILD HALL WAS on Main Street in the center of East Hampton, a pretty village divided by a narrow canal and an ancient burial ground. The cemetery, which had been there since the 1600s, lent a certain gravitas to the shops and restaurants that sprang up like toadstools after rain and were mowed down just as quickly. The taste for delicacies from Provence and fat-free yogurt might wax and wane, but Lion Gardiner, stretched out on his tomb like a medieval knight, was eternal.

The lobby of Guild Hall was solid with bodies, a mélange of beautiful people discovering each other with little cries, kissing the air beside each other's heads as if afraid of disease. More than once I heard the words, "Truly a sad occasion." Not all of the men had on tuxedos—several were wearing beautifully tailored dark suits—but I was sure that even the shortest, skimpiest dresses around me cost more than a Hemingway first edition. This was the kind of occasion that my twin sister, Patience, and her husband, Ben, who had a summer home in Southampton, would try to be seen at. We didn't share information about our social calendars though.

"Think Pat and Ben will be here?" I asked Colin.

"I wondered about that. I haven't seen them in a coon's age."

On several easels near the auditorium doors were photographs of the Eriksons. One, from a Beaux Arts Ball, showed them recreating the painting of Spanish royalty, *Las Meninas*. Nate, as the artist, Velázquez, wore a black mustache and held paintbrushes, and Eve was a beautiful Queen of Spain, her black hair shining under a coronet. Puck, in a rust-colored velvet suit with a lace collar, was the little boy with his foot on the dog in the painting. A pretty little girl as the golden-haired princess in an elaborate ivory dress with a huge skirt could only be Regan. Bianca hovered over her along with Rosa, who in adult makeup was perfect as the dwarf. Gretchen was the adult attendant. Only a gawky Claude standing beside Eve, dressed to look older and represent the king, took a leap of imagination.

A copy of the original painting has been posted for comparison, and it was uncanny how well the Eriksons replicated a portrait painted over three hundred years ago. Only the dog was missing.

Another exhibit showed scenes of Hampton life, with Nate playing in Artists vs. Writers softball games and posing in a group with Eve at a picnic on the beach. The last board held pages from the *Life* magazine story Bianca had mentioned, photos of a younger Nate in his studio and walking the grounds. One photo showed the whole family around a table, drawing. An adorable Puck, no more than two, held a fistful of crayons up to the camera.

I didn't see my sister or any of the Eriksons in the lobby, so we continued into the John Drew Theater and found our seats in the fourth row. The auditorium was opulent, with a silky tan and brown ceiling and a crystal chandelier. A grand piano, shrouded in canvas, was discarded on one side of the stage like somebody's aunt. Looking around, I located Eve shifting restlessly between Bianca and Claude, fingering her program like a small child forced to sit still in church. Lynn, wearing a ruffled black dress, was beside her husband. Rosa on her left looked half asleep.

Oddly, there was an empty seat between Lynn and Rosa, as if the family did not want to be identified with her. Then I realized it was not odd at all. The empty seat was the one they were saving for Gretchen. She must be still in the lobby talking to old friends. Claude stood up then and scanned the room as if looking for her. His oversized tuxedo hung from his shoulders like a jacket draped on a scarecrow. I was certain that it had been Nate's, that by wearing it Claude was hoping to be the man his father had been.

I stared down at my program feeling the weight of Colin beside me. I looked calm but was churning inside. I had no doubt he *did* love me. But why did Henry Higgins and Eliza Doolittle come to mind?

A chime trilled three notes, and the rest of the audience wandered in gracefully. When everyone was seated, a smiling dark-haired woman approached the side podium. She was dressed in an ivory silk suit, perhaps to show that she was a member of the staff and not a guest.

"'In the midst of life we are in death,'" she said softly. "But a wise man once reminded us that there is a season for everything. For living, and for dying. We are in mourning for this great artist who was taken from us so tragically. Yet we are also gathered here to celebrate his extraordinary talent and life. Nate Erikson did not live in vain."

Briefly she described how he and Eve had come to Springs in the early 1970s as a young married couple, raised a family, and helped to develop an entire artistic community. "They called their home Adam's Revenge and it was indeed paradise on Earth. Only the privileged were allowed inside. Their presence in the community triggered the migration of other artists, especially to Amagansett and Springs. And all of this before the Hampton Jitney."

A ripple of surprised laughter.

"Nate Erikson will be remembered most for the illustrations that enriched the lives of readers the world over. Tonight we are privileged to have an exhibit of his landscapes as well as the work of his daughter Regan, a talented artist in her own right. Most excitingly, unlike our museum exhibits, these works are available to collectors," she finished demurely. It reminded me that the money from the tickets, besides any commissions from sold artworks, went to benefit Guild Hall.

The speaker introduced Regan next, and I sat up to get a better look at the sister that everyone hated. Her fair hair had darkened to chestnut and tumbled over her shoulders like a stream breaking on rocks. Her silky dress of beautiful patchwork colors was either an expensive designer creation or a vintage store offering. There had been nothing like it at Veterans' Thrift or I would have snapped it up.

"I grew up before the term 'dysfunctional' was applied to families," she began.

There was an intake of breath around me. At last people would be hearing the true story of what went on behind those garden walls.

"But it wouldn't have mattered. My childhood was an idyllic one."

A release of disappointed air.

"My father, whom we are honoring tonight, taught me everything I know about creativity. My mother taught me what I needed to know to get by in life. I never went to an art school, never went to *any* school. I had a classical and individually tailored education, as did my brothers and sisters. They have all chosen creative fields. And though *my* children are being educated more conventionally, I am confident they will carry on their grandparents' tradition."

"Not those little bastards!" Eve's voice rang out in the stillness.

Consternation, everyone in the first few rows turned to stare. I saw that Claude was smirking, Bianca staring down into her lap. Lynn had her hand up to her mouth. Gretchen's seat was still empty.

The buzz from the back of the auditorium was probably everyone else trying to find out what Eve had said.

"I see my mother hasn't lost her sense of humor," Regan continued with a grim smile. "But we're here tonight to honor my father. Clyde Still, an artist you all know and one of my father's closest friends, wants to say a few words. And then you'll be hearing my brother's music. So I won't take up any more of their time."

She stepped down to vigorous applause.

CLYDE STILL SAID what he would be expected to say in warm remembrance of Nate Erikson, his colleague and good friend. Simple words, yet they fixed Nate in a specific time and place. His words made me imagine Nate a single figure in the circle of a spotlight. He had had his time on earth, lived wholeheartedly, and was not allowed a second more. I stole a glance at Colin to see if he was feeling what I was. In profile he looked thoughtful, perhaps pensive, but I didn't know what his thoughts were. I was still too upset to lean over and ask him.

As soon as Clyde Still left the stage, we were plunged into darkness. When the footlights shone again, Puck, another young man, and a young woman, dressed identically in black turtlenecks and black slacks, were standing behind a row of objects on the table. I looked at my program and saw the piece was called "Beach Reverie."

The three musicians moved skillfully, clanging on a tin sand pail, continuously dropping stones into a glass container, and beating a piece of driftwood with a stick.

There was a background recording of gulls shrieking over the roar of waves, and, periodically, a mournful ship's whistle. The sounds from the table were miked loudly into the room.

Of the six pieces, my favorite was "Toy Shop." The live instruments were a wooden toy piano painted white, friction cars that Puck zoomed across the table, and blocks stacked, then knocked down with a clatter. An old cloth-bodied doll wailed, "Ma-ma" when she was flipped upside down. The background music was busy and staccato.

Unlike Clyde Still's eulogy, this had not been expected.

After some dutiful applause—no one yelled "Bravo"—Colin nudged me. "You brought me here for *this*?"

He was teasing, but I felt responsible. "No, I brought you here to meet Bianca Erikson. But it's late, we can go." I was feeling in no mood to socialize. I needed to replay our dinner conversation, hold it up to the light and consider its implications, before I made any decisions. I planned to sleep on the way back to Port Lewis.

"No, no, I'll talk to her."

For Bianca's sake, I led him into the next room.

CHAPTER SEVENTEEN

I'D EXPECTED TO see the family standing in a receiving line to greet old friends, but they had already scattered into the crowd. Glancing behind me I thought I saw Charles Tremaine, and felt clutched by cold fingers. He would approach Eve, offer to buy Nate's books, and there would be a terrible scene. Guests would learn something new about the Eriksons after all. But when I looked again, I couldn't see him.

Bianca was standing near the bar, stylish in a sleeveless black sheath, her gingery hair in waves around her face. She looked sad and alone, her eyes red, but she managed to smile when she saw us.

"Delhi. Don't you look sweet. I didn't even know you with your hair up. You look like a friend of mine."

Did she mean I looked like someone she could be

friends with, or someone she already knew? Probably the latter; it would take more than a blue velvet dress to make us equal in her eyes.

"Where's Aunt Gretchen?"

"I don't know! When it was time to leave, she still wasn't back from her errands and we couldn't wait any longer. But she had one of the cars, so we assumed she'd come on her own."

"But she didn't?"

"No . . ."

Colin couldn't keep out of the spotlight any longer. "Colin Fitzhugh," he told Bianca with his disarming smile. "I understand you write poetry too."

I had planned to slip away and look at the paintings on the walls once they were engrossed in each other. Truth be told, I couldn't bear to watch Colin weaving his magic for yet another woman.

I had turned to go when I heard an incredulous voice. "Delhi?"

I turned and saw my sister, Patience. She was also wearing royal blue, but her dress had more sophisticated tucks and folds, and her diamond necklace was real. Still, with her blond hair in the French braid she always wore, we looked like a page from *Vogue* showing dresses by the same designer.

"Hey, Pat. I thought I might see you."

"What are you *doing* here?" She sounded as if I had been attracted by the lights and wandered in.

Then she saw Colin, and her eyes widened further.

In our last conversation, sometime in the summer, she had commiserated with me about my marriage being over.

He moved over to kiss her on the cheek. "Lovely as always, I see."

"Hello, Pat," Bianca said, stepping into the conversation with a professional smile. "I didn't realize you knew each other."

That was too much. Patience looked heavenward, and I started to laugh. "We're sisters," I said. "Fraternal twins. I guess I didn't tell you I had a twin."

"Separated at birth," Bianca agreed. But when she saw I wasn't teasing, she looked from one to the other of us more carefully, then shook her head at me. "You're married to Colin Fitzhugh. You and Pat Selzer are *twins*. Oh, I know. Your father is Warren Buffett."

"He's sorry he couldn't be here."

Pat pulled at my arm. "I think I need a drink,"

The others laughed, as people always do when they hear that.

We moved to the table where two bartenders in white dinner jackets were taking orders. I picked up a flute of champagne and Patience ordered a mojito.

Once we had our drinks, she got me alone in the hallway from the theater and turned accusatory. "You never told me you knew Bianca Erikson."

You didn't tell me you were married to Colin Fitzhugh. Why were connections so important to these people? "You never cared who my friends were before."

"That's because they were nobodies. This is different. Bianca Erikson? And where did you get that dress?"

"You like it?"

"I don't know. What are you doing here with Colin? Are you back together?"

"Not really." I accepted an oyster wrapped in bacon from a passing tray. "It's complicated. Bianca wanted to meet him, she's a poet too. Tell me something." I glanced around to make sure no Eriksons were in hearing distance, then pulled Pat closer. "How did Bianca's husband die?"

"He's dead? My God, when did that happen?" I hadn't seen her so shocked since someone put a snake in her locker in junior high.

"Last March?"

"You mean Jack Marshall? He's not dead, he's living in Sag Harbor! He and Bianca are divorced. He already has a fiancée."

Marshall had been Morgan's last name in the news clipping.

Patience shook my arm. "Why did you think Jack was dead?"

"I don't know. She said that she had lost him and I thought he had died too."

"Not as of last week."

I lowered my voice further. "Speaking of Colin, he made me a crazy proposition."

"He's gotten kinky?"

"No." I couldn't help laughing at the thought of him handcuffing me to the brass bed. "He has this idea that he wants to buy a grand manor now that he's been made division head and he wants me as his official hostess. I mean his wife. Whatever."

She pressed her glass against her mouth to hide a laugh. "What would your duties be?"

"The usual. Decorate the mansion, entertain, play nice with his colleagues. The kind of stuff *you* like. No books, of course."

"But he knows you'd never agree to that. Why would he even suggest it?"

"I don't know." Had Colin thought I would refuse, leaving him free to do what he really wanted? Did he have some young woman hidden on the portico? Maybe he and Bianca would hit it off; she'd be the perfect hostess. The champagne glass felt cold in my hand.

"The trouble is, you two are too much alike."

"Alike? Colin and me?"

"Don't look so outraged. You both want to do exactly what you want. You're both sure you're right. You were just lucky that for a long time you wanted to do the same things. Anyway, you should consider what he's suggesting. I worry about you living hand-to-mouth, eating cat food in your old age."

"*Our* old age. I could come and live with you like a maiden aunt. Raise the children."

"By then they'll have children of their own. Listen, I have to circulate."

And she was gone.

I TOOK THE chance to look at Nate's paintings. They were all landscapes, showing the fields behind his house, the bay at low tide, and other scenes I could not identify. I was disappointed. They were too impressionistic, lacking the sharp details that made his illustrations so memorable. They might have been painted by any local artist.

On the other hand, I would have admired Regan's work even if I hadn't known who she was. Her paintings were simpler, the clean lines and flat areas reminding me of Fairfield Porter. Some of the objects were deliberately oversized, giving a fresh perspective—a baby bottle, a cheese sandwich, a bowl of fruit. A painting of a tan crock of huge red geraniums would have looked perfect in my barn. I squinted at the price: forty-five hundred dollars.

As I straightened up, I turned and saw Regan Erikson studying me. I hoped she didn't see me as a prospective buyer. Next to her were two bored-looking boys around six and eight. The standard-bearers of the next Erikson generation. Or, if Eve was right, the little bastards who would squander their heritage.

Keeping an eye on the boys was a slender Japanese man. He reached over and smoothed the younger boy's hair.

I caught my breath. Was he the reason they were not welcome at the compound? Eve had fiercely condemned the Japanese, and Puck had explained that his grandfather had been captured and killed during World War II. What underlying currents would have made Regan marry someone who was anathema to them? *An idyllic childhood gone sour.*

With her eyes still on me, there was nothing to do but walk over.

"I love your paintings," I said. "I wish I could afford one."

"You and the rest of the world. Are you local?"

"No, I'm from Port Lewis. Delhi Laine." Without thinking, I took a business card out of my woven bag, one that showed a photo of my Siamese cat, Raj, standing on a stack of books. As soon as I handed her the card, I realized my mistake. Bianca had instructed me Thursday afternoon not to say anything to Regan about the books.

"What's *her* objection?" I'd wanted to know.

"I don't even know if she has one. But we thought it best not to involve her."

Which meant that Regan wouldn't be sharing in the profits either.

"Bianca and I are friends. She wanted me to hear Puck's music."

"What did you think of it?" The man tending the boys moved into our conversation.

"Actually, I kind of liked it."

"This is my husband, Dai Harada. You do know the performance was a put-on? Puck's always been like Kokopelli, a trickster, he has the oddest sense of humor. My father indulged him way too much. But it's hard to accomplish anything serious on the compound."

"Was that why you moved?" As soon as the words slipped out, I was sorry. Far too personal a question to ask someone I had just met.

She shot a quick look at Dai, who glanced away, embarrassed. "We lived there for a while when we were first married. But when we had children, I wanted them to have a normal life."

It wasn't what I was expecting to hear. Had I gotten everything wrong? Maybe she was estranged from the family *because* she had left. Maybe the estrangement had nothing to do with her husband's race.

"Don't get me wrong, I had a fascinating life."

"I'm sure."

"If you'll excuse me, I have to find my aunt." Her eyes searched the crowd beyond us.

Should I tell her Gretchen wasn't here or let her find out on her own? I decided it wasn't up to me to say anything.

"She isn't here," Dai said quietly. "I looked."

She turned on him. "What do you mean she's not here? She has to be here! Where's Bianca?"

She spun around, but Dai put his hands on her shoulders. "No scenes."

"They aren't going to get away with this!"

"Yes they are. We'll sort it out later."

"How? Someone needs to blow this family sky-high."

"They will. But not you. Not tonight."

CHAPTER EIGHTEEN

On Monday Bianca was waiting for me on the parking gravel. She seemed to be headed to one of her committee meetings, beautifully dressed in suede slacks and a matching turtleneck in rich chestnut brown. A gold medallion encircled her neck. "Thanks for bringing Colin Saturday. It helped me get through the whole awful thing."

"He enjoyed meeting you. The memorial was lovely." It was the kind of thing I was expected to say and "lovely" was a word no one could argue with.

"Don't expect much for lunch today. It will only be sandwiches."

"That's what most of the world eats." When she didn't respond, I added, "Gretchen has the day off?"

"No, she never came back! I mean she *did*, the car was here when we got home, but she never came down for breakfast yesterday. We think she must have gone to Regan's."

I remembered Regan's frantic search for her at the memorial. Maybe she had visited the house before the family got home and spirited Gretchen away.

"She didn't leave a note?"

"No. Sorry, I have to go." She started toward an older tan Lexus.

"Did you call Regan to check?"

"And give her the satisfaction? You don't get it, do you?"

Now she did walk away.

FOR THE FIRST time since I'd begun evaluating the books, the morning dragged. I sorted through the art theory and reference books Nate had amassed over the years. Most were common printings and not worth much. I bundled them into lots of three or four but still had to check their value.

The ham and cheese sandwiches that accompanied the deli macaroni salad had been assembled by Bessie, who pointed out firmly that cooking and serving were not what she'd been hired to do. Washing dishes wasn't part of her job description either.

Nate Erikson was toasted, rather glumly, with tap water.

Eve was the one who spoke up. "What a bunch of sad sacks you are! I can't believe that not one of you had the gumption to go into the kitchen and prepare a proper meal. Bessie's right. We need to make new arrangements. Until Gretchen comes back, you girls can take turns doing the shopping and cooking. The boys will do the clearing up and load the dishwasher. And what about *you*?" She pointed at me and I wondered if I would be assigned table setting. "I want to see your artwork."

My artwork? Then I remembered I was supposed to be illustrating Bianca's book of children's poetry. *Be sure your sins will find you out.* I've never been able to get away with a single thing. There's a practical reason why I don't rob 7-Elevens.

Now I had an image of staying up all night trying to copy illustrations from obscure children's books. But I discarded that quickly. Why should I be lured into something dishonest? Then I remembered my tinted photographs from England. They were old, they weren't drawings, but at least they were mine. "I'll bring some tomorrow."

"See that you do. If you're doing something as important as illustrating my daughter's book, your work has to be top tier."

At this point it was barely bottom drawer. I felt Bianca shift anxiously beside me.

"How soon do you think Gretchen will be back?" Claude broke in.

"As soon as she remembers she's lucky to have a roof over her head," Bianca snapped.

I blinked, shocked. She was talking about Gretchen, the woman who had raised her. Then I realized how hurt she must feel that Gretchen had gone over to the enemy without even leaving a note. She hadn't said good-bye or told them when she would be back.

"She still has to take care of her garden." Rosa spoke up unexpectedly. "And I have her things."

"What 'things'?" Claude demanded.

Instead of answering, she reached for more macaroni salad.

"Maybe Gretchen just needed a rest," Lynn said. "Cooking for seven people every day is hard work."

"What seven people? There are only six of us." Bianca was still ready for a fight.

"Yes, but she had this annoying habit of wanting to eat sometimes herself," Puck said.

Bianca glared at her brother. "You're such a smart ass."

"At least I don't write people off."

"That's right, you're Mother Teresa. I never saw *you* offering to give her a hand."

"Regan just wanted her own cook," Claude grumbled. "She didn't have to steal ours."

Lynn turned on her husband, appalled, her fair cheeks flushed. Martha Stewart about to confront a cheeky audience member. "For God's sake, we're talking about someone in your family, not some indentured servant you inherited along with the manor. The trouble is, none of you think about anyone else's feelings."

Eating cold food was making people testy. After that the conversation withered and died.

WALKING BACK TO the studio with Bianca, I asked, "Gretchen didn't tell you anything?"

"If she had, we'd know where she was, wouldn't we?"

I noticed that more trees were starting to turn color.

"You think we're heartless. But there's a lot of history

here you don't understand. You have something more important to worry about anyway. What kind of pictures are you going to show my mother?"

As if claiming to be an illustrator had been my idea. I had a friend like Bianca in fifth grade, a fat girl with freckles who blamed me for everything in her life that went wrong. A bad geography grade, a spilled juice box, her dog dying. We weren't friends by sixth grade.

"I have some photographs of children I hand-tinted."

"Don't you know any artists?" She turned it into one more failing.

What had happened to our closeness on Friday? Did she think she had said too much, been too vulnerable, and was pulling back now to reestablish a proper distance?

"I don't know anyone who illustrates children's books. It's a niche market." *Sorry, Maurice Sendak.*

"My fault, I guess. I thought I'd have time to get a real illustrator. I should have said you were here to make curtains and slipcovers for the cottage."

Oh, wonderful. "And you'd invite your seamstress to have lunch with you every day?" I didn't bother to hide what I was feeling.

"Only if she was good enough." Bianca started laughing at her own absurdity and reached out and patted my arm. Then I was laughing too.

IT TOOK ME two hours to locate my photographs stored in the basement. There were not many that would work for a children's book. Most of them were shots of the English countryside, marshy riverbanks and thatched-roof cottages. I picked out two that looked poetic. One showed an old mill churning water into a stream. The other had been taken at night with the moon over a Cotswold village.

There weren't as many pictures of my children as I remembered —what kind of a mother had I been? *Dangerous territory.*

I set aside one of beautiful blond Jane absorbed in a book, and one of Hannah and Caitlin, mirror images, exchanging daisies. I only let myself think for a moment what Caitlin would be like now. *More dangerous territory.* There were several tinted photos of the girls before England, one a favorite that did make me cry: the three little girls in Easter coats and bonnets, clutching toy rabbits that my mother had given them. My mother, now gone herself. I was surprised not to find any photos of Jason, then remembered that I had given up taking pictures in the weeks before he was born.

For the past two weeks my lost child Caitlin had been in the shadows of my mind. It was as if I had been hearing my name called and spinning to find no one there, just an outline of air where she should have been. I'd had to brace myself to look at the photos. I would be opening a locked door and looking at something that was forever lost.

I WOKE UP in the middle of the night, certain that Gretchen would never have left the compound without putting her garden to bed for the winter.

CHAPTER NINETEEN

"YOU BROUGHT THE pictures?"

Bianca came into the studio while I was setting up my computer for the day.

Silently I reached into my woven bag and handed her the brown envelope.

She pulled the photographs out, frowned, and scanned them quickly. Then she laid each one on the worktable. As a group, they were pathetic—clichéd landscapes, clichéd children, the pastel tint faded. But she'd said she would be finding a real artist anyway.

After a moment she turned to me wonderingly. "These are beautiful—exactly what the book needs! Who knew? Meeting you this way, it must have been karma. Do you have other photos? Can you do more?"

I was stunned by her reaction. I had never anticipated that they would be anything other than a stopgap measure. "Are there still darkrooms? It seems like everything's digital now."

"I'm sure you could find a lab online. Digital has made black-and-white photos into an art form. Acrylic paints never replaced oils." She began collecting the photos, holding each one carefully by the corners, and returned them to the envelope. "Let's show Mama!"

"Now?"

"Why not? She's up at the house."

"What do you think she'll say?" I was surprised by how strongly I wanted Eve to like them too.

"We'll find out."

EVE WAS SITTING on an overstuffed sofa in the great room, legs crossed, reading *Art in America* magazine. "Lucien is showing at Acquavella again," she told Bianca. I couldn't tell if she felt vindicated or aggrieved by that. For a moment I was surprised to see her reading *Art in America*—but why not? Despite some occasional confusion, her intelligence had never been in doubt.

"Delhi's brought her illustrations to show you," Bianca said. "I'm very excited about them." Excited, but I saw she was also biting at her lower lip.

I handed Eve the manila envelope and watched as she extracted the photos.

She scanned them rapidly, then thrust them away like an advertising circular she had no interest in. "These are photographs! What Nate did, those were book illustrations. Bianca, you must find a real artist." She pointed a bony finger at me like a fairy tale witch. "This one must leave now."

"Mama, that's silly. These are just what I was looking for."

I told myself Eve was reacting that way because they were photographs, not because of their quality. Wishful thinking, but I said, "Maybe you've never heard of Toni Frissell."

"Toni? I knew Toni. What about her?"

"She did a beautiful book of photographs to illustrate *A Child's Garden of Verses* and one of Mother Goose rhymes. They're considered classics."

"She photographed her children." Her face softened. "She brought me a quilt when we moved here. She was as old as my mother." Then she glanced at my photos again. "Are these your children?"

"Some of them." I meant some of the photographs, but either interpretation was true. There were no pictures of Jason.

"Well, do what you like," Eve told her daughter. "It's *your* book."

She said it the way someone might say, "It's your funeral." Bianca gathered up the prints quickly and we left the room.

When we were outside she said, "You'll need to read my poems, so you can figure out what other photos we need."

"Your mother wasn't enthused . . ."

"Don't worry about her, she's just upset over Gretchen. They had tea every afternoon and now her routine's disrupted. Who's this Toni person, anyway?"

"Toni Frissell? She started out as a fashion photographer, then went on location during World War II as a photojournalist. She took a lot of pictures of the Tuskegee Airmen. After the war she did some beautiful black-and-white photographs for books."

"Tinted like yours?"

"No."

"Well, I like yours better. When did you take them?"

We started down the front steps. The blue hydrangeas drooped, but the black-eyed Susans bloomed on.

I put my hand to my face as if the pressure would make me remember. "Fifteen years?" I don't know why I said that. I knew exactly how long ago it was.

"Is your recent work different?"

"There *is* no recent work."

"Why not?" She picked up the scent immediately.

"It's a long story. A sad story."

"Tell me."

I was ready. If anyone could understand what had happened and how I felt, Bianca would. After we returned from England without Caitlin, we had never told anybody what happened. The tragedy had been packed away with the tiny toddler dresses, never to be talked about. Now unpacking time was here.

But as we came around the corner we saw Rosa struggling with an oversized coffee table, half out of the trunk of the old tan Volvo.

"God in heaven spare us," Bianca muttered.

The coffee table did not look heavy, but it seemed awkward for one person to get a grip on. As we got closer, I said, "Let me help you."

"Don't!" Bianca commanded, but I was already moving toward Rosa.

The table was the type that had probably been popular in the 1970s, with leather squares on the top and tooled in gold around the edges.

"Can you believe someone put this out with the trash?" Rosa asked me, her dark eyes incredulous.

"It just needs a little work," I agreed.

"No, it doesn't! It's perfect the way it is."

I helped her maneuver the coffee table out of the car, and between us we carried it to its new home.

THE CLUTTER OUTSIDE Rosa's chalet seemed worse than a week ago. I saw a new tower of empty Easter baskets on the porch, their pink and green wicker sides crushed as if stomped on by petulant children. A cartoon-eyed rabbit had joined the flock around Snow White. I wondered if anyone had thought about taking away Rosa's car keys.

"Where are you going to put it?" I asked.

"I'll find a place. Come in, I need to give you something."

I followed her into the living room, wedging myself into an opening on the couch between tottery stacks of clothing.

Rosa pushed aside a tower of magazines and sat on the piano bench opposite me. Suddenly she thought of something and turned to burrow on the upright piano top, finally unearthing a brass-framed photograph. The brass had been tarnished by time.

Nate Erikson, wearing an ermine cape, had his arm around a small girl in a tutu with angel's wings. Her gap-toothed mouth was opened in delight.

"That's you?"

"Me and Dad, at a Midsummer's Night party. I miss him a lot. And Aunt Gretchen. They were the only ones who ever—" But her dark face looked as if she was unwilling to finish the sentence. "Something bad is going to happen," she whispered.

"What do you mean?"

"I hear noises outside at night. Someone is trying to get in and hurt me." She pushed up and disappeared into a side room.

I waited on the sofa, feeling oppressed by the multitude of objects everywhere, the ghosts of people now disappeared. I couldn't think of a way to describe the subtle energy that radiated from them, other than as the heat that sunburned skin gave off. Against the far wall several unframed canvases were stacked together and I got up to look. Did Rosa paint, as well as do ceramics? The canvas facing me was of a woman with long black curly hair wearing a white blouse and a red shawl around her shoulders. She wasn't anyone I could identify by name and yet I knew I had seen her before.

Then Rosa was back, and saw me looking at the portrait. "That's my mother. My *real* mother. Gretchen painted it before the train . . ."

"She's lovely. *Gretchen* painted it?"

"She put her name there."

The "Erikson" had blurred with time, but I could make out the G.

Then Rosa had hold of my arm. "You have to hide this for me." Her voice was a dramatic whisper. "You can't look at it unless something bad happens to me. Do you promise?"

I took the legal-sized white envelope from her and slipped it into the manila envelope of photographs. "I promise. But I'm sure you'll be fine."

Unfortunately, it wasn't the first time I had been wrong.

CHAPTER TWENTY

THE PHOTO ROSA had shown me nagged at me all afternoon. What bothered me was its similarity to the picture of Nate and Morgan that had been burned. Had Rosa come in, seen the photo on the worktable, and incinerated it in a fit of jealousy? Because she, and only she, could be Nate Erikson's fairy princess?

I was packing up for the day when there was a soft knock on the door and Bianca stepped into the studio. "I brought you my poems."

"Great. I'm looking forward to reading them."

"Are you keeping track of the time you spend here?"

"Of course." I gave her a figure, glad that the subject had come up. I badly needed to be paid.

"That's about what I thought. We decided we'd keep a running total and reimburse you when the books were sold. Okay?"

I blinked at her. But this was what rich people did.

They ran a tab, and since you wanted to seem as cavalier about money as they were, you agreed. Sometimes the money never materialized and there were lawsuits.

Either I had to align myself with gracious living, or tell Bianca how I really felt.

I chose the low road. "I need to get paid," I said. "Now."

Her face closed like a morning glory at sunset, consigning me to the great unwashed where she had first assumed I belonged. Was this the end of my book appraising career? Even if it was, I had no regrets. What I had learned about illustrated books and Nathaniel Erikson's milieu was priceless.

She eyed me to see if I could be intimidated, then said grumpily, "You want a check *now*?"

"That would be great."

A stagy sigh as if she had hoped for better from me. *The revolt of the working classes.* "I'll have to get a check from Claude. It may take a while."

Was he going to argue with her too?

"It's only five. I can wait."

"No, close up here. I'll meet you at your van in ten minutes."

Bianca took much longer than ten minutes. An early evening haze was starting to blur the farthest hills when she returned. "Here. Is this good?"

I looked at the slip she handed me through the window. The amount was exactly what we had agreed on. "Thanks." *Long Island Power Authority thanks you too.*

As Bianca headed back toward her cottage, I noticed the signature on the check: Eve Erikson. But how—then

I decided that Eve herself had not signed it. Was Claude his mother's executor? Had she agreed he would write checks on her account to pay for household expenses? What would she say if she saw one for over a thousand dollars made out to her daughter's collaborator?

Get this puppy to the bank.

WITHOUT OPENING IT, I put the envelope Rosa had given me in the glove compartment under a collection of maps and repair bills. I wondered if it was something Gretchen had given her for safekeeping, something that Rosa was now afraid she would not be able to protect. The sounds she was hearing at night were probably no more than the deer so endemic to this part of Long Island or raccoons foraging in the garbage. Subconsciously she was probably worried about Gretchen.

Where *was* Gretchen now? I could accept she was at Regan's, but why hadn't she come to the memorial? She had had her suit cleaned and planned what she was going to say. Even if she hadn't been on the program, they would have been happy to let her speak. If she had been in an accident . . . But all three cars—the Lexus, the Toyota, and the battered Volvo station wagon—were on the gravel circle.

I was worried enough to call Regan Erikson that night. The number was listed under "Harada, Dai" the only one in Kinderhook.

One of the boys answered and I asked for their mother.

"Mommy, there's a lady on the phone."

The receiver clunked onto a table, and then a scraping as it was picked up again. "Hello?"

"Regan, this is Delhi Laine. I was the one who admired your work and talked to you at the reception. Bianca's friend?"

"I remember you."

"I should have told you that the reason I know the family is because I'm illustrating a book of Bianca's poems. So I'm out at the compound a lot."

If a silence could go cold, this one did. "You're an artist too?"

"A photographer."

"Here I thought you were just a book dealer."

So she had read my card. "It's not *just*. I love books, they're what my life is about. There's not a big market for tinted photographs anyway."

"So you're like an actor who waits tables."

She hadn't been listening.

"The reason I'm calling is to make sure Gretchen is with you. Bianca would kill me if she knew, but Gretchen left so quickly and didn't leave a note or anything . . ."

"With me? Why would she be with me?"

"Well, nobody's seen her since before the memorial."

"What are you talking about?"

"Gretchen went off to do an errand Saturday afternoon and never came back. I mean she did, the car was there, but she wasn't. Would anyone else have picked her up to take her to Guild Hall?"

"How should I know? This doesn't make any sense. I have to talk to Dai. What's your number?"

The phone rang fifteen minutes later. "I'm coming down tomorrow morning to find her. Something's happened. Maybe she hit her head and wandered off into the woods. She could be lying there unconscious!"

"You're going to the house?"

"Where else?"

"They don't know I called you," I warned.

"Don't worry, I won't say anything. At least you cared enough to phone. I'll tell them the truth: that I got worried when I didn't see Gretchen at the memorial. They know I stay in touch with her. Will you be there?"

"Probably."

"See you tomorrow then." She hung up.

I clicked off too, feeling uneasy.

It was time to read Bianca's poems.

CHAPTER TWENTY-ONE

When I got to the compound I went straight to Bianca's cottage. She opened the door wearing a silky pale blue robe with matching pajamas, cinched tightly around her narrow waist. "I didn't go up to the house for breakfast," she said.

"I wanted to tell you that I'd love to do the book illustrations." Seeing my photos again had been like coming across a forgotten love letter and realizing the feeling was still there.

"Oh. Great." But her voice was flat and I wondered if she was having second thoughts.

"I read your poems last night. I think they're wonderful." Strange, anyway, certainly not what people would consider poems for children. And yet their undercurrents, their oddity, were feelings children would understand. One kept repeating in my head:

> *The old woman outside the fair*
> *Told him it was a lie.*
> *"Nobody sent you those postcards," she said.*
> *"They dropped down from the sky."*

Bianca brightened at my praise.

I was hoping she would offer me a cup of tea and keep me out of the studio awhile longer. I hadn't told Regan I was working in that sacred space and didn't know what she'd say if she found me there.

But Bianca turned toward the back of the cottage, probably to get dressed, and I started for the door.

My hand was on the knob to leave when there was a pounding on the other side. *Regan already?*

I braced myself for a scene.

Bianca moved past me to open the door.

Instead it was Bessie who half-fell inside, her face contorted. "Miss Bianca, there's a woman up at the house, says she's looking for your aunt."

"A woman?"

"She *says* she's your sister. She's after upsetting Miss Eve!"

"Oh, for God—let me get some clothes on and I'll go back with you." Bianca turned to me, and I saw from her expression that she hoped I would come too. It only took her a moment to pull on jeans and a white turtleneck under a navy V-neck sweater. Her ginger hair was a cloud around her face.

As we climbed the hill, Bianca cross-examined Bessie. "Exactly what did she say?"

"We was in the sitting room, when I heard someone banging at the front door. I went to see, and this lady said she come to see her Aunt Gretchen. I said she wasn't here, and she pushed right inside." Bessie was gasping now with the exertion of climbing. Beads like clear jewels had appeared on her dark forehead. "I kept saying Miss Gretchen wasn't home, and then Miss Eve came out.

"*She* says, 'What are you doing here? You get out of here!' But the other one kept saying, 'What have you done with Gretchen?' I thought I better get you." She gave a worried look at the house.

Bessie sounded sincerely upset, and yet . . . Miss Eve? Miss Bianca? This wasn't Birmingham in 1952.

Send me Hattie McDaniel from Central Casting.

Bessie turned her head then and looked at me. She didn't smile, yet there was a look of amusement in her deep brown eyes as if I had caught her out.

We climbed the porch steps quickly.

MOTHER AND DAUGHTER turned as we came into the living room. I was surprised at how little resemblance I saw between them. Eve with her white hair and creased face was older, of course, but her facial structure was delicate, more refined. Today Regan was wearing a beautiful multicolored mohair sweater and jeans, her hair tamed into a ponytail. What struck me was how beautiful both women were. They might have been actresses rehearsing for a play.

"What's going on?" Bianca demanded.

"She's poking around where she's not welcome. She knows she's not allowed here."

"You didn't even call me when Dad died! I had to find out from the news."

"But why are you here now?" Bianca interrupted. "Isn't Gretchen with you?"

"Why would she be with me? She'd never go off without telling you, you know that."

"Then how did you know she was missing?"

Uh-oh.

"I didn't. But she never would have missed the memorial and my art show. I came down to find out why. Then I find out you don't even know where she is!"

"Because we thought she was with you."

I kept expecting Eve to jump back in, but she was watching her daughters calmly, as if they were squabbling teenagers.

"You searched her room?"

"Of course. Her bed hadn't been slept in. We didn't know she was gone until Sunday because the car was back."

"Which car?"

"The Toyota."

"That old wreck's still around?"

Eve came to life at that, pointing at Regan, nearly jabbing her chest. With her white hair and bony finger she looked unearthly, a Shakespearean wraith. "You. Go away now."

"Oh, shut up, you old witch." Regan pushed her

mother's hand away, then moved toward the door. "I'm going to look outside."

Bianca turned to Eve. "Are you okay, Mama?"

Eve flipped her hand at her, as if dismissing an underling.

CHAPTER TWENTY-TWO

ON THE WAY back to Bianca's chalet, I learned why Regan
was persona non grata.

"Why does your mother hate Regan so much?"

"Hate her? She doesn't hate her. She's her *daughter*."

"She sure doesn't want her around."

We had reached the chalet and Bianca migrated to
one of the yellow rockers on the small stoop. I sat down
in the other.

"Mama's never been that warm and loving . . ." Her
voice trailed away as she perhaps realized the gap between not showing affection and ordering your child off
the premises.

I waited.

"It's mostly about money. When Regan decided to leave
she demanded what she called her inheritance. Dad gave it
to her finally, but my mother was furious. No matter how
much money there is, she takes it personally if any goes to

anyone but herself. I think it was Gretchen who pressured him into doing it.

"Actually, it's *all* about money. When the rest of us wanted our share to do things too, the bank was closed. My father just laughed and said we'd have to wait till he was gone. Now he's gone and my mother's worse than he was. At least he gave us an allowance."

"And she doesn't?"

"Well . . ."

I remembered that Claude was good with a check-book.

We rocked.

"I thought maybe it was because of Regan's husband being Japanese."

"Dai?" She gave a short laugh. "That was the icing on the cake. He was our *gardener*. So the wedding wasn't exactly the social event of the year. The irony is, Regan's doing better than the rest of us now. Financially, I mean."

But not emotionally. We saw Regan hurtling toward us as if being chased by a serial killer. We jumped up at the same time and ran to meet her halfway.

Her face was white. She opened her mouth several times but nothing came out.

"What is it?" Bianca cried.

Regan pointed mutely in the direction of the pool.

We couldn't get her to tell us. When her teeth started to chatter, Bianca said, "Go back to my cottage. We'll look."

The grass felt wet through my sandals and made me wish I were eight again, faced with nothing more complicated than how to spend a beautiful fall day. I didn't want to see what had shocked Regan. I hoped it was a dead animal that Regan hadn't gotten close enough to identify.

We moved through an opening in the archway of cedars and onto the tile surround. But the pool looked the same as the other day. Only the water sprites and mermaids, so lively then, now seemed sinister.

"There's nothing here," Bianca said.

"Wait." I moved to the edge of the deep end and looked down. The sweet, meaty, metallic smell ambushed me before I saw anything. Breathing through my mouth, I saw what Regan had.

I put out my arm to hold Bianca back, but it was too late. She came up beside me for a moment, then made a gagging sound. Overcome by the stench, she rushed out to the grass. I heard her being sick on the other side of the hedge, and waited until I thought she was finished. It was less out of delicacy for her feelings and more because the sight of someone vomiting is contagious. I was taking quick, shallow breaths through my mouth myself.

When Bianca was quiet again, I steeled myself and stepped through hedge arch back to her. "Are you okay?"

"Okay? Are you kidding? How can anything ever be 'okay' again?"

CHAPTER TWENTY-THREE

REGAN WAS HUNCHED over on the sofa, arms between her knees. Her head jerked up when we came in. "Was that *Gretchen*?"

Bianca went over and sat down next to her. The sisters held each other tightly like shipwreck survivors.

I leaned against the door, then went over and dropped into the chair opposite them. I felt as weak as if my body could blow away—the way I had felt in Port Lewis several weeks ago when a fast-moving car hadn't seen me in the crosswalk and slammed on its brakes, stopping less than an inch away. The car was so close that I could feel the heat from the hood and at first I thought it *had* struck me. I barely made it to the other side and collapsed on the curb, pressing my head dizzily against my knees. The people around me had rushed to help as the car sped away.

Now we sat in silence, trying to understand what we had seen.

"It must have been the wheelbarrow," Regan croaked finally.

I stared at her. That had been no wheelbarrow in the pool.

"What wheelbarrow?" Bianca whispered.

"Gretchen's wheelbarrow, the one she always used in the garden. It was lying on its side above where . . ."

"You think she tripped on it?"

"How else did she fall?"

It brought the image I had been trying to suppress fully back. A crumpled navy sweat suit with a snake of white seam along the leg, an arm thrown out uselessly, a bloated, blue-tinged face bobbing in the filthy water. Strands of golden hair, a familiar color.

"We have to call someone," I said.

Bianca looked at me, then gave her head a shake. "You're right. I'll call McConnell's."

"Who's McConnell?"

"The funeral home who—"

"I mean you need to call the police."

"But it was an accident!"

"This is private property," Regan added. "It happened on private property."

"No police. No way." Bianca was implacable. "We're not having the police here again." She moved as if to stand up, then dropped back onto the couch.

I couldn't believe what I was hearing. I knew how upset they were, but what were they thinking? Next they would be planning to dig a grave and bury Gretchen themselves.

"I know someone I can call," I said.

"You mean a lawyer?"

"No, a detective. He's with Suffolk County."

"Which word didn't you understand, Delhi—'no' or 'police'?"

"Someone has to move Gretchen. The funeral home won't do that."

"Of course they will."

But I was fishing around for my woven bag and I found the phone inside. Frank Marselli's number was in my list of saved contacts from the Old Frigate case, and I pressed "Dial" quickly.

He answered as if he had been waiting for my call. "Marselli."

"Um—hi." One of those horrible moments when you forget your own name. "This is Delhi Laine. I don't know if you remember me, but—"

"How could I forget you, Ms. Laine?"

It wasn't exactly the tone of someone with fond memories. When he had been investigating the deaths at the Old Frigate Bookstore, he had often seemed exasperated and infuriated by me. On the other hand, his integrity was unimpeachable.

I tried to talk quietly. "I'm in Springs and my friend's aunt has been missing for three days. We found her in a pool with a little water and it . . . looks bad."

"They don't have police in the Hamptons?"

"I know. But they don't want to call anyone. It's complicated."

"It always is with you, isn't it? You're lucky I have to be out east later today for another case. Call the locals, use

911, and don't touch anything! Where are you, anyway?"

I gave him the exact location, then said good-bye.

"He's coming." I slid my phone shut. "By himself." I didn't pass on the rest of his message.

Regan pushed up from the couch. "I'm going home."

"Home? You mean back upstate?"

"Where do you think? I need my family."

"He'll need to talk to you."

"You talk to him. I have to pick up my kids from school."

It was 10:30 a.m. "But you were the one who went looking for Gretchen."

"So what? He's your friend."

Frank Marselli was hardly my friend. In July he had acted as if I were a plague inflicted on innocent police officers. What was the opposite of romantic interest? Although divorced, he was obsessively devoted to his kids and his job and would have done nothing to jeopardize either. That was what made him trustworthy.

"I don't want to talk about it." She gave me a mulish glare and stood up.

"Are you okay to drive? Why don't you wait awhile and calm down."

"I'm fine, okay? They don't want me here and I don't want to be here. Especially *now*."

"I don't want you to leave," Bianca said.

"I said no."

I watched Regan open the door and disappear, knowing I couldn't make her stay.

Bianca moved to her desk. She pulled open a dainty

desk drawer and took out what looked like a memorial card. Then she picked up the cordless receiver and moved toward the kitchen.

After three or four minutes she came back in and slammed the phone into its holder.

"What did they say?" I asked.

"They need a doctor's note first."

"A doctor's note?"

"A death certificate. Whatever."

I never say, *I told you so*, but the words seemed to hang in the air.

"So what happens now?"

"You have to tell your family."

"Tell them what? We don't know anything for sure."

Well, we know that Gretchen won't be making lunch.

BIANCA COULDN'T SIT still. She wandered around her pretty living room, touching knickknacks and repeatedly straightening the small landscape painting over her desk. One of Nate's? "I can't take this in. Every time I forget it for a minute then remember, it's like being slapped all over again. When I was little I loved Gretchen better than my mother. Regan still does. It's funny, but Gretchen was the only one who *didn't* think Puck was adorable. She hated his tricks."

Was Gretchen's death part of a prank that had gone horribly wrong? Maybe Puck had lured her outside to frighten her, and the joke had turned tragic. "When are you going to tell them?"

"When we—ohmygod, I'm supposed to do lunch! I completely forgot about it."

Who could worry about lunch now? "Can't you order pizza or something?"

She stared at me. "Pizza? You think this family eats *pizza*?"

The picture of them using their hands to munch on slices in that formal dining room almost made me laugh. "McDonald's cheeseburgers then. Except no, McDonald's doesn't deliver."

She didn't understand that I was teasing her. "My family has only ever had home-cooked meals for lunch. Lunch is our big meal. Mama would die if I brought in pizza. Or cheeseburgers."

"People won't feel like eating anyway when they find out."

"Oh, they will. They'll be sad, but they'll eat."

I couldn't believe that. If someone that close to me died so horribly, I'd never want to see food again. Even now the thought of trying to swallow anything made my throat close in protest.

"What's something like pizza, but that everyone would think I made?"

"Sushi?"

"Really? Does that go with Caesar salad?"

I gave up and prayed that Frank Marselli would get here soon.

CHAPTER TWENTY-FOUR

I MANAGED TO get Bianca out on her front porch to wait for Detective Marselli, but I couldn't persuade her to go up and tell her family. I knew why she dreaded doing it, knew that telling people would make what happened real and set the family on another grief-stricken journey. Perhaps a guilt-filled one as well. Why *hadn't* anyone gone looking for Gretchen?

I hadn't realized how close to the edge I was until the police-issue navy sedan screeched into the gravel area and I slumped back in the rocker. "That's him."

Bianca sighed and pushed out of her rocker. "Let's make this quick."

She still didn't get it.

We had nearly reached the car when Claude barreled out of the house and down the steps. "You can't park there. This is private property!"

"I don't doubt it," Marselli said easily.

I couldn't understand what had provoked Claude's outburst. Marselli was wearing pressed khaki slacks, a pin-striped shirt, and a navy blazer. His olive skin was smooth, his buzz cut trim. With his clipboard he looked like a building inspector.

"You'll have to leave."

"Claude—" Bianca began.

"Oh, I don't think so," Marselli interrupted, smiling. He wasn't always in such good humor. "I was invited. Suffolk PD." He took out a black leather case.

"You're from the police? Did my sister send you? She thinks something's happened to my aunt. Nothing's happened to my aunt."

Marselli gave me a puzzled look.

"Claude, we *found* her." Bianca finally finished her sentence. She moved over to him and held his sleeve. They started to whisper intently.

"So what's the story?" Marselli asked me, as if we had just seen each other the day before.

"She's down in the pool. The thing is, she's Nate Erikson's cousin."

He didn't react.

"The illustrator? Like Norman Rockwell? You've heard of him, you must have. The family is *famous* around here."

"Your point?"

"Everyone thought Gretchen had gone off to visit one of her nieces, so no one was very concerned. But then that niece, Regan, came looking for her, and found her body— I'm not sure how—"

"Are the locals here?"

We were walking down a slope of grass that had already lost its dewy luster. From this angle the pool was still blocked from view.

"No, they wouldn't let me call anyone. They wanted to shuffle her off to the funeral home." *Or bury her on the back forty.*

"The funeral home would have set them straight."

"They did. But the Eriksons aren't like most people. They're terrified of bad publicity."

"Not that unusual."

He stopped as Bianca and Claude caught up with us and the opening to the pool came into view. "In there?"

I nodded.

"Stay back." Marselli stepped away from us and pulled a thin pair of vinyl gloves from his pocket. He put them on and glanced up the hill past the garden to the house, staring at everything for so long that Claude impatiently pushed past him to the edge of the pool. When I caught up with him, he was already staring down.

"My God," he croaked. "Is that Gretchen? It's not her—it's just some old clothes someone threw in."

Except for the twist of golden braid.

Marselli waved us away and I stepped back, glad to get farther from the nauseating smell. Once again I was breathing through my mouth.

Claude seemed frozen in place for a moment, then twisted away and retreated to the other side of the cedars.

Marselli walked to the shallow end and started down the tile steps into the pool. I noticed that he didn't touch the metal railing for support. Moving slowly, he finally reached the navy shape and knelt beside it. I stepped forward enough to see him lift her head out of the water. Then he was doing something to her face, perhaps examining her eyes and mouth. I looked away.

On the other side of the hedge I found Bianca, lips as thin as a ruled line, arms tightly crossed as if trying to keep warm. Claude was rocking back and forth on his heels, looking gray. They paid no attention to me.

Marselli came out several minutes later. Without looking at any of us, he reached into his inside pocket and took out a cell phone. Then he moved away and started talking.

Bianca grabbed at my arm. "Who's he calling?"

"Probably the medical examiner. Someone has to sign the death certificate. You know that."

"Why can't *he* do it? Gretchen fell and hit her head. It's not rocket science. Look, there's the wheelbarrow Regan was talking about."

I looked up and saw its red metal cradle half covering a bush.

Marselli snapped his phone shut and stalked over. "Who found her?"

"My sister Regan," Bianca said.

"She's in the house?" He looked up. From here it seemed to stretch for stories.

"No, she went home. She lives upstate."

"She went home?" His earlier good humor spiraled down the drain, leaving the detective I had come to love. "She left?"

"I told her she had to stay, that you needed to talk to her." I felt like a tattletale, but I didn't care.

"She had to get home for her kids," Bianca said defensively.

Oh, please. "Those kids are in school."

"She's always been irresponsible," Claude said. He had morphed from lord of the manor into concerned citizen. "Always wants to blame everyone else."

I wasn't sure what that had to do with this situation.

"But any of us could have found Gretchen," Bianca protested.

"Why are you defending her?" Claude was outraged. "You know what she's like."

"How come your sister from out of town was the one who found her? Didn't the rest of you realize she was missing? A family member disappears for several days and you don't notice?"

Bianca looked slapped. "We thought she'd gone off to my sister's in Kinderhook."

"The same sister who found her? Did she do that often?"

"Sometimes."

It had to be a lie. If Gretchen was expected to cook every day, she would have had to make arrangements to be away. Her not doing so was one more red flag.

I shivered in the sunless day.

"Okay, wait for me in the house. Stay indoors and don't wander around. For now I'm treating this as a crime scene."

"Just because we didn't look for her?" Claude cried.

Marselli waved that away. "Because we don't yet know how she died." He pulled out his cell phone again and waited for us to leave.

As we moved toward the main house, Bianca yanked at my sleeve. "I thought you said he'd take care of things quietly. He's turning it into a circus!"

"He has to find out what happened."

"We know what happened. She tripped and hit her head. It's a terrible thing, but she was old and probably got dizzy."

Claude turned on us. "Whose bright idea was it to call the police?"

"Hers." Bianca jerked her head at me.

"Oh, come on! The funeral home said you had to call the police."

"No they didn't, they just said we needed a doctor's note."

Please excuse Gretchen Erikson for being dead.

"This is going to kill Mama," Claude said.

I didn't know if he meant Gretchen's death or the return of the police.

CHAPTER TWENTY-FIVE

THERE WAS NO sitting down to a normal lunch after that. At Bianca's request I went into East Hampton and bought back a fruit and cheese platter, chicken salad, and bread. Grimly she arranged everything on the coffee table in the great room as if creating an intricate work of art. No pretense of iced tea today. Claude brought out several dusty bottles of red wine that were emptied immediately.

Nobody talked. We might have been strangers waiting to board the same plane. Through the open window I could hear vehicles skidding on the gravel and pictured officers going about their various tasks—photographing Gretchen's body, examining the area for physical evidence, preparing to move her to the morgue for the autopsy. A policewoman was already in the house going over her room. Claude, still in cooperative mode, had signed a consent form for Gretchen's room to be searched.

Marselli had explained that the local police had to be

involved, that as a detective from the Homicide Bureau he might or might not be staying on the case.

It seemed odd that he didn't warn us not to discuss what had happened among ourselves. Evidently that caution was only on TV procedurals, although the patrolman standing inside the door was a deterrent to any collusion. We had been told not to leave the premises, though only Bessie and I had anywhere else to go. She was sitting on the couch, looking grave, her big hand clutching Eve's slender one. Eve wasn't saying anything, but seemed to know what was going on. Puck, facing away from us in a recliner by the window, was paging through the *New Yorker*, occasionally sipping his wine and chuckling over a cartoon. The rest of us sat like patients awaiting a bad diagnosis.

"Where's Rosa?" I suddenly realized she was missing. *Something bad is going to happen to me.*

The family looked at each other.

"I guess nobody told her," Bianca said. "She gets so involved in what she's doing."

"I'll get her." Claude bounded up from the love seat, jostling Lynn. He seemed happy to leave the room.

CLAUDE AND ROSA had been back for ten or fifteen minutes when Marselli finally appeared in the doorway. I was relieved to see that Rosa was unharmed. I had expected her to be upset, perhaps weeping, but she seemed to have turned any emotion she was feeling in on herself. Her expression was stony above her paint-smeared blue smock and she didn't speak to anyone.

As soon as he saw Marselli, Claude was on his feet. "What's going on?"

"Early days. They're still investigating."

"What's to investigate? Do you always investigate domestic accidents this way? Or is it because of who we are?"

Marselli eyed him. "According to the medical examiner, this was not a natural death."

I had wondered why the police were searching Gretchen's room.

"What does *that* mean?"

I held my breath. Marselli did not take well to belligerence.

"It means Ms. Erikson did not stumble into the pool and hit her head. She was dead before she ever went outside."

The whole room seemed to inhale.

Claude rallied first. "Then she must have had a heart attack. Or suffered an embolism."

"Maybe. But she didn't put herself in the pool."

"She could have fallen in by accident. Maybe she was looking at something that scared her so much her heart gave out."

Evidently he hadn't processed the information that Gretchen died indoors.

Marselli frowned, as if he had used up his supply of civility. "I'm not officially on this case yet. I said I'd get some background. Where's a good place to talk?"

Silence. Lynn opened her mouth, then closed it again.

Finally Bianca said, "I guess you could use the dining room. It's on the other side of the hall."

"Okay, good. Ms. Laine, come with me please."

Everyone looked startled. Surely I knew less about Gretchen than anyone else. This wasn't an Agatha Christie novel in which I was her long-lost daughter given up for adoption, come back to wreak revenge.

I followed Frank Marselli back into the hall and led him to the dining room. He sat at the head of the table in Eve's chair, and I sat down on his right.

"Odd ducks," Marselli commented.

"I think they're more upset than they let on. Why do you think Gretchen didn't die in the pool? She could even have drowned."

"She didn't drown. Lividity shows she was lying on her back and wasn't moved for several hours. She probably died in bed. From the look of her eyes and mouth, I'd say she was suffocated, but the ME won't confirm that yet. The only reason I'm telling you is because I need some help with these people. One of them has to know what happened. What are you doing so far from home?"

I told him about the book assessment, what had happened to Nate Erikson and Morgan, and about Gretchen's odd position in the family.

"Did you ever have a conversation with Ms. Erikson?"

"Yes. We talked about her vegetable garden."

"And?"

"She loved it, but was still in mourning for Nate and Morgan. She didn't seem to feel that cooking for the family was demeaning though. She and Eve Erikson had tea every afternoon."

He drummed his fingers on the beautiful cherry table. "So everybody loved this lady."

"The girls more than their brothers, I think. But there is one thing. She said she had an important announcement to make at the memorial for Nate on Saturday night, but that she had to check something out first. And no one ever saw her again. She wasn't there to say what she had planned."

"Where does their money come from?"

It was a good question. "I think Nate Erikson earned most of it. He was paid well for illustrating the books, and he sold the paintings they were based on for a lot more, especially in the seventies and eighties. I think Mama owns the bank now. According to Bianca, the kids need money and she won't give them any." Should I tell him about Regan and the controversial inheritance? That seemed too complicated and tangential.

"But Mama wasn't the one who was killed."

"No."

"And there's no mistaking the two women. Did Gretchen Erikson have money?"

"I doubt it. Where would she get it? As far as I know, she's lived here since the kids were little, and never worked. She may have inherited money from her own family, but in that case, why hang around?"

"You tell me."

"I don't know. It *was* her home. But she only had one room in the main house, not even her own cottage like the kids. Regan didn't stick around anyway."

"The missing sister? What's her story?"

I looked over at Nate Erikson's portrait. "She's estranged from the rest of the family. I was the one who called her. Gretchen didn't seem like the type to go off without telling anyone. She was—I don't know—too mellow. So I called to check. The family would kill me if they knew I contacted her."

"My lips are sealed. You're saying the only reason Ms. Erikson was found was because this sister came looking for her?"

"Well, no one else was looking." It was chilling to think of Gretchen lying there, decomposing into something less and less human until . . . "But you can see why they might think that. Regan was down on Long Island for the memorial last Saturday when Gretchen disappeared."

"You think she had anything to do with it? She knew where the body was." He wrote something in his notebook. "Another reason for the skedaddle home. So what's your theory? You always seem to have one."

But I didn't, not yet. "Can I think about it?"

He swept a hand toward me. "You can do anything you want to, Ms. Laine."

An improvement. In the past he had treated me like one of those pesky kids, a cub reporter or amateur sleuth, hanging around the pros and whining, *What's going on? Huh, huh?* Now he at least considered my ideas.

ONCE I WAS dismissed, it didn't feel right to go back to the studio and research books. How could I, haunted by the image of Gretchen's body crumpled and motionless? I didn't want to sit with the family either, so I went into the great room to say good-bye to Bianca.

She jumped up when she saw me and walked me to the front door. "What did he ask you?"

"Oh, you know. He wanted to know who lived here. I told him no one had ever left except Regan. If you have other missing brothers or sisters, tell me now."

She laughed. "But what you said isn't technically true. Claude and Lynn were gone for a year."

"Really? Where'd they go?" To peddle Paper Pusher in Japan?

She sat down on the front steps, and after a moment I did too.

"Claude finally insisted on going to college. He always loved science, he'd had his heart set on MIT or somewhere, but my parents wouldn't allow it. They said college would be a 'waste of his creativity.'" She gave me a droll look. "Like he had any. They were really afraid that if he went off, he wouldn't come back."

"He seems very bright."

"He's brilliant. He's constantly researching things on his own. So my father finally agreed and Claude and Lynn went off to Rochester. RIT." She rubbed absently at a spot on the wooden tread. "It was a disaster. Maybe because he'd never been to school and had to sit in class, but he failed everything. There was no point in his going on, so they came home and Claude went back to his Rube Goldberg 'inventions.'"

"That's so sad."

"It was. The only bright spot was that they had missed Peter, their son. The agreement was that he would stay at Hampton Day, and Gretchen would supervise him."

"Your parents held Peter hostage?"

I meant it as a joke mostly but Bianca said, "Oh, don't be so dramatic. It was the best arrangement for everyone. But Claude's serious about inventing things now. That's why he's so anxious to get the books appraised and sold, so he can set up a real lab. My father wouldn't hear of his building anything on the property, but he sees this as his chance."

Good luck getting it past Eve.

Bianca pushed herself up. "I'll see you tomorrow?"

"Same time, same place." Hard to believe that it would be only Thursday. "Do you want me to try and order film over the Internet?"

"Wait on that. We need to sit down with the poems first. Do you have more tinted photos of children?"

I knew I didn't, but I said, "I'll look."

CHAPTER TWENTY-SIX

I WAS CURIOUS to know what the police had found out, but Thursday morning I didn't see anyone to ask. There were no unfamiliar cars in the circle, no activity that I could see around the pool. If it hadn't been for Marselli's observations about how he thought Gretchen had died, I would have concluded her death had been a tragic accident after all.

I was almost to the studio when Bianca burst out of her chalet. She didn't even say hello. "I don't know why I ever let you call that jerk. Those policewomen were in Gretchen's room for *hours*, they claimed someone had ransacked it. *They* were the ones who tore everything up. Then the ambulance took Gretchen without even telling us. I've never seen such a lack of consideration. They should all be taken out and shot." From the set of her head, I saw she would be happy to line them up and fire away.

I didn't know what to say.

"Any policeman from around here would have seen Gretchen lying in the pool and known it was an accident. We'd already be planning her memorial service."

"I doubt the police around here are *that* dumb."

We glared at each other. "What are you saying? Out here they know the family! They know none of us would hurt Gretchen. The East Hampton police would never have taken our fingerprints—they even took Bessie's. They would have taken yours too if you'd been here. I wish you had been."

I smiled. The police had fingerprinted me in July after the murder in the bookshop.

"Anyway, I'll see you later. For lunch."

There was something ominous about the way she said lunch, but for Gretchen's sake I had to go. I needed to watch these people. To listen. One of them had smothered Gretchen in her bed.

WHEN BIANCA CAME to get me she was still on edge.

"Whose turn is it to cook?" I asked.

"No one's. I mean, someone from the outside. Bessie's granddaughter, Jocasta."

"Jocasta?"

We started up the hill. The blue hydrangeas had nearly faded to white.

"What—you think only a Harvard PhD can name a child after a Greek myth? That black people aren't entitled?" She shook her head. "Talk about racial profiling!"

Jocasta, the mother of Oedipus, was actually a character in a play by Sophocles, but I wasn't going to correct Bianca. Today she would have insisted the earth was made of pizza dough.

As usual, we were the last ones into the dining room. Bessie was standing against the wall behind Eve, a large presence with an anxious smile, her muscular arms pressed against her sides.

A beautiful, lighter-skinned young woman, her hair in a hundred skinny red-gold braids, wheeled a cart through the archway. When she efficiently transferred its contents to the sideboard, I could see fried chicken, mashed potatoes, green beans, and cornbread.

"Fried chicken was my husband's favorite," Eve said to me, as if I were about to challenge the meal. "This young woman is schooled in the culinary arts."

"It's my favorite too." Nobody did fried chicken better than KFC either, but today I was watching what I said.

It was time for the toast.

"To Pa," Bianca said quickly, her glass raised.

"Never forgotten," Claude intoned.

"And to Gretchen," Lynn's clear voice rang out. "May she never be forgotten either!"

If she was expecting a fight, she didn't get one. The others murmured their agreement and lowered their eyes. I still didn't know what to make of Lynn. Did she find living on the compound confining? Or did it free her up to follow her bliss?

"This is very good." Lynn smiled over at Jocasta.

It was good, but I didn't think this young woman had much to do with it. I identified the mashed potatoes as coming from Boston Market. Probably the chicken came from there too, along with the overstewed green beans. The cornbread tasted like my favorite Jiffy mix.

"So what exactly is your relationship with this cop?" Claude demanded across the table. Everyone else stopped eating and looked alert.

"No 'relationship.' I got to know him when he was investigating the murders at a bookshop in Port Lewis, and I knew the people involved. I think he's good at what he does."

"*I* think he's a pain in the ass. Did he catch anybody?"

"Yes." With a few prompts and—okay, a few hindrances—from me.

"Are you wearing a wire?" It was Puck. Before his attack on Bianca the other day, I would have written it off as a joke.

"No wire. I'm as much a suspect as anyone else." *Bad choice of words.* "I mean, he questioned me too."

"Why? You didn't know Gretchen."

"Well—I've been out here a lot. I told him I didn't know why anyone in the family would want to hurt your aunt."

"Of course we wouldn't," said Lynn. "What we need is a better alarm system."

Ah. "The alarm didn't go off?"

"No, and it should have. Unless it went off when we were at the memorial. But no one came to investigate."

"That we know of," Claude corrected her. "They may have stopped by and found everything in order."

"The police can check if anyone was notified," I said.

Except that Marselli had told me Gretchen had lain on her back for several hours before being moved. Few intruders would wait around to do that.

Jocasta entered then with dessert, a stack of unpeeled bananas and Entenmann's chocolate chip cookies. Bessie jumped forward to help her clear the lunch plates.

"Oh, don't do that," Eve cried. "You do too much for me as it is." It was the most affectionate thing anyone had said since we sat down at the table.

CHAPTER TWENTY-SEVEN

THE AFTERNOON PASSED quickly in the studio. I had finished with Nate Erikson's books and the association copies inscribed to him by other artists. Many of those were exhibition catalogs, published by art galleries. I suspected that some of the novels in the bookcases were autographed as well, but I was saving them for Monday. First I had to finish my spinach, the ordinary art books that could be sold as small lots. I reminded myself that I should be interested in Nate's sources of inspiration—a well-thumbed *Gray's Anatomy*, Kimon Nicolaides's classic on drawing, and *The Science of Color*—but I kept thinking about what had happened to Gretchen instead.

I had explained to Bianca that I wouldn't be out there tomorrow, Friday, because of a book auction I wanted to attend, so I decided to celebrate the end of the work week early. I would veer east and stop at one of the seasonal clam bars near Montauk Point before they closed for the winter. The farm stands were already displaying tiers of orange and yellow mums, and pumpkins had been spread on the ground for a week. Many homes had their wooden porch rails hidden behind papery cornstalks and their doors decorated with Indian corn.

I was envisioning a lobster roll, a glass of white wine, and finally settling into *Let the Great World Spin*, when I pulled out onto Cooper's Farm Lane. Then I heard a car start up behind me. Damn! It had better not be Charles Tremaine. It was, of course, and I couldn't ignore him. I had promised him updates in return for his backing away quietly from the Erikson books. But why did he have to choose tonight, when all I craved were a few creature comforts after a shocking week?

I beeped once to let him know I knew he was there.

We went back to Flaherty's. Already the room seemed less crowded than the week before. The Hamptons' season of packed restaurants and vacationers was falling off, and I wondered how many customers this bar attracted on a Thursday night in January. It seemed too upscale to be the neighborhood hangout, and too substantial to close down in winter like the clam bars.

"White wine?"

"Chardonnay. Thanks." We returned to the same table we'd sat at before. Above my head the Dos Equis mirror reflected a warrior's profile between two red Xs and I wondered how often people chose the same place they had sat at the last time. I was imagining other instances where that might be true—doctors' waiting rooms, movie theaters, classrooms, church pews—when Charles came back carrying my wine and his scotch.

He slid his lanky frame into the chair. "I hear you had some excitement at the Farm."

"Is that what people call it, the Farm?"

"Mostly people who remember the original owners, the McCarthys. It's hard to believe, but residents were scandalized when Nate moved in and made all those changes. They were sure he was just another crazy artist come to destroy the area."

"And then they found out how sane he was compared to Jackson Pollock."

"They did. But it seemed sacrilegious that he was tearing down the old farmhouse and barn and putting up new buildings. Never mind that the old ones were falling-down wrecks." He looked amused. "I'm on to you, missy. You're cleverly steering me away from the topic of what happened yesterday."

I took a sip of the wine. "Why do you think something happened?"

"Because there were Suffolk County police cars and an ambulance at the house? Because they took someone away covered by canvas? And no"—he held up a hand—"I wasn't there watching. As you reminded me last time, I have a business to run."

"How did people know?"

"Do you live in the twenty-first century or are you lost in a book somewhere? Cars go down that road. School buses go down that road. Cops talk to each other. I'm sure the Eriksons would like to think they live in a bubble, but in our electronic world that's impossible."

"So you already know what happened."

Charles hesitated. His startling gray eyes looked away from me and then back. "It was a woman, from what I understand."

"Which one?"

Now he smiled. "That's what you're going to tell me."

I drank more wine.

"Just tell me one thing: Was it Eve?"

"No."

"One of the *girls*?"

"If I tell you, you'll tell everyone else."

"No. I won't. Cross my heart and hope to die," he intoned. It was the first time I had seen a man in his sixties make that X across his chest. "I raise my right hand up to God," he added whimsically, lifting his palm. Someone standing at the bar laughed.

I thought of something. "There was a painting of a young woman in the studio, with hair like mine." The painting I had been terrified I had destroyed, the one that someone else had tried to destroy before I ever saw it.

"It was *her*?" The glass in his hand slipped a little.

"Who is she?"

"What do you mean who—she wasn't the one who died?"

"No."

"Then why did you mention her?"

"I'm curious who she was."

"How should *I* know?"

But I knew he did.

"Trade," I suggested.

"Okay. You first."

I thought about what to say. As soon as the coroner released Gretchen's body and the family planned the funeral,
people would know anyway. I was surprised no journalists
had found out. That would change. "It was Gretchen."

"Gretchen." His tone implied respectful surprise. "You
know, she was someone I never 'got.' She looked like a
German hausfrau celebrating Oktoberfest, she wore these
blond braids coiled around her head, but she was what the
kids call *hot*. She didn't go light on the schnapps either."

"Gretchen?" I didn't doubt his comment was true,
he had no reason to make up about stories about a dead
woman. But it was a different Gretchen than I had seen.
"Did she ever get serious with anyone?"

"Not that I know of. What happened to her?"

"She fell."

"These household accidents are killers. That family
has the worst luck."

"Your turn."

He smiled. "I told you, I don't know anything."

I put down my glass. "Yes, you do. Your face when I
mentioned my hair."

"They had a babysitter who kind of looked like you.
Younger of course. Sonia. But I never knew her last name
or what happened to her."

Again I was sure he was lying about that.

Then I realized the significance of what he had said.
He was the first to mention that Sonia, the au pair, had
had hair like mine. Was she the girl in the slashed painting, the one that Eve had mistaken me for at lunch the
first day? It seemed odd that she would be posing nude,

especially since that was not Nate's usual type of art. Had something been going on between them?

Charles was pressing on. "What's happening with the books?"

"They'll probably go to auction." A childish way of getting back at him.

"So I don't get any breaks for knowing Nate?" He took a final sip of scotch.

"Not unless you want to offer fifty thousand up front. When I give the family the true value, I'll tell you. You can make them an offer."

"But they'll expect top dollar! I *never* pay that, I couldn't afford to. Besides, it would mean I'd have to take all the books."

"I thought you said the library shouldn't be broken up."

He grinned. "I did say that, didn't I? But no library stays together forever, not even Thomas Jefferson's. I mean, I'm sure Nate had some wonderful books, and others not so good. So why pay for ones I don't want? I have a sophisticated clientele."

"No reason you should have to," I agreed.

"On the other hand, to be so close to those books all these years, then have to bid for them at auction like everyone else? It doesn't seem fair."

Poor baby.

"It's not like the family needs money," he argued.

"How do you know? Who doesn't need money these days?"

"You think? Well, maybe. Taxes alone on that place have to be in the stratosphere. And who's bringing in money now? Surely not those kids." He made them sound like a bunch of layabouts, deadbeats with hayseed stalks between their teeth.

"They aren't lazy," I protested. "They all do some kind of art. They were raised to think that money isn't that important."

He laughed. "It will be if they ever run out."

I changed the subject. "Are you going to the Phillips auction tomorrow?"

"Of course. Don't tell me you are."

"Why not?"

But he wouldn't be lured into insulting me. "Because you have better things to do."

"I've got to run," I told him. "I'll call you when I'm done at the Eriksons."

"Sounds like a plan." He stood up when I did, and extended his hand. I took it, surprised at the formal gesture. No doubt it was the way he treated his "sophisticated clientele."

It was too late for a lobster roll and I didn't want to drink any more wine. Instead I contented myself with a small strawberry shake and a cheeseburger from McDonald's, tamping down my guilt with the thought that a Big Mac would have been even less healthy. Colin, of course, would be scandalized. His idea of fast food was a carefully arranged platter of sushi.

CHAPTER TWENTY-EIGHT

NEARLY A WEEK after the memorial I was still not in the mood to think about Colin and what he had said at dinner that Saturday night. How could I consider moving back in with someone who wouldn't promise that we would grow old together? Someone who wouldn't assure me that if I gave up the life I had made for myself he wouldn't change his mind again? I turned it around. Suppose he had promised undying love: Was I really ready to give up my independent life and the bookselling that I loved and step into the pages of *Gracious Living*?

The sense of alarm I felt when I came through the back door into the kitchen and saw the message light blinking gave me the answer to that.

My faithful cats, Raj and Miss T, came running to greet me. I scooped Raj up, burying my face in his fur. I gave Miss T her turn, then snapped open a can of Fancy Feast for them. Finally I pushed the play button on the machine. There was a blank buzzing that meant a robo-call from a charity, and then my daughter Jane in Manhattan. I was surprised. She rarely used the landline.

"Hi Mom, it's me. I wanted to ask you something. Anyway, call me on my cell, I don't know where I'll be by the time you get this."

I picked up the cordless phone and went into the living room. Despite a struggling economy, Jane, at twenty-four, had managed to hang on to her financial services job. And why not? She was beautiful, engaging, and a wizard with money. I had tried to keep her from turning into Patience, though I hadn't succeeded. She had the same sense of how people of a certain class should behave, and the same desire for an astronomical income.

It wasn't until I sat down in Colin's suede wingback chair, which, surprisingly, he hadn't taken with him, that I wondered with a sudden flare of dread if Jane had called because she had been fired. That would be unthinkable, yet things like that happened even to superwomen like my daughter.

Her phone rang several times and I waited for it to go to voice mail.

"Hi, Mom."

"Hey love. How are you?"

"Great. How are *you*?" She cut to the chase. "Have you talked to Dad recently?"

"Last Saturday we went to dinner and a concert in the Hamptons. Has something—"

"Did he say anything about leaving the condo?"

"Well, he talked about buying a mansion, and installing me as his hostess."

She snorted. "But what about your books? Your books are what you do. I told him if he forced you to give up the barn, I would never speak to him again. And I won't."

"What? When?"

"Last night."

I was stunned. She was the only one of the children who could give Colin such an ultimatum and have it stick. She was his amazing daughter, the relationship he would never jeopardize. Her gesture brought me close to tears. "Thanks, babe."

"So what's all this about a mansion?"

I reminded her about Colin's promotion and added that he felt his new position warranted a suitable home to entertain in—as well as someone to keep the silver polished. I knew I was being unfair. He was older than I was, fifty-five to be exact, and I understood that after all the temporary housing we had lived in that he might want the security of his own home. Perhaps in ten years I would feel that way too.

"Now he's becoming conventional? After all these years of dragging us all over the globe? Are you considering it?"

I hesitated. How much of your personal life do you share with your kids? They were there for a lot of the drama, but saw it through the filter of what they needed from you. Unless you deliberately made them your confidants, they didn't know everything that went on in the dark. "Let me say this," I began.

But then I stopped. Children believed, deep down, their parents belonged together. How else could they ever enjoy a family Christmas again?

"We're still sorting it out." That was certainly true.

"He talked about moving. But I told him there's nothing wrong with the farmhouse. You could fix it up and entertain there."

"He wants to own something." The idea of Colin, the *size* of him, back in the space I had gotten used to as my own, felt like someone shoving me into a corner.

"Listen, Daddy doesn't need a grand manor any more than my boss needs a red Bugatti. As I keep telling him. Men of a certain age . . ." She let her voice trail off.

I laughed. "Men of a certain age are men of a certain age." *Deal with it.* "While I have you on the phone, I want to ask you something. Do you remember when we were in Stratford-upon-Avon?"

"A little. We've been so many different places."

"Do you remember anything particular that happened there?"

"Mom, I was a baby."

"You were four."

"That's where Shakespeare lived, right? Anne Hathaway's cottage?"

"That's right, but—"

"Whatever. Gotta run. Meeting Bryce in ten minutes."

"Bryce? What happened to Lance?"

"History. Tell you later. Love you."

"You too." But I was talking to a dial tone.

So Jane didn't remember. She *hadn't* been scarred for

life by repressed memories. Even though she didn't love books the way I did, even though she was as ambitious as Patience, she had a life that made her happy. Jason, the child who was struggling the most, hadn't even been born when we lost Caitlin. Maybe we had been right to bury the tragedy and move on.

And yet—I replayed our conversation, chasing down the nuance that kept evading me. After I brought up Stratford, Jane had sounded different, slangy and breezy, her answers clipped. And then she had quickly ended the conversation. I knew she was telling the truth about not consciously remembering anything. But something still frightened her.

CHAPTER TWENTY-NINE

FRIDAY MORNING I didn't take the train to Manhattan and attend the Phillips auction. Charles Tremaine was right. Who was I kidding? Maybe ten years from now . . . I had thought it would be an education, seeing rare books that I could never afford to buy even as investments. But now taking the time seemed foolhardy when I had so much to do. What difference did it make to me if a first edition went for eighteen thousand dollars instead of twenty thousand dollars? *I* wouldn't be bidding on it. Instead I went to a large library sale in Nassau County and came away with a satisfying collection of art books and children's series.

On Saturday, though the season was nearly over, I left the house early to attend a smattering of sales. The first one seemed to be a wash, oversized toddler toys and ugly china, but when I examined the table of books and CDs, I spied an early copy of Howard Garis. Grabbing the book,

I saw it was a first edition of *Uncle Wiggily on the Farm*. I flipped through to look at the illustrations— my pleasure plummeting when I saw that a juvenile artist had decorated the pages with a green crayon. I started to put the book back down, then decided that the six color plates might be salvageable.

It's a better practice to buy several books instead of one—otherwise sellers tend to be suspicious that you have discovered something priceless—but I couldn't honestly see any other books that I could bear to carry home. So I brought *Uncle Wiggly* up to the card table where a man about my age was engrossed in conversation on a tiny cell phone. While I waited, I studied his graying buzz cut and a paunch that stretched out the Marine insignia on his shirt. He ended his conversation and snapped the phone shut.

"Ya want that?"

"How much is it?" Most books at yard sales aren't marked. There is usually a blanket price of fifty cents or a dollar.

He took the book and flipped through it. "Thirty-five dollars."

"What?"

"Thirty-five dollars."

"But it's got crayon scribbling all over it!"

"I know. It's mine."

Don't insult him, Delhi. "That's a little high for me."

"Okay then, thirty. But I can get more than that on eBay."

Just try it.

"So? Take it or leave it."

I left it.

I drove away, thinking evil thoughts about ex-Marines.

AT THE NEXT sale, I was walking up the driveway when I saw the Hoovers, Susie and Paul Pevney. They were loaded down with several cartons each. They hadn't been nicknamed the Hoovers by other booksellers for nothing. Unfortunately, the books they vacuumed up at the end of sales were worth about that.

The Pevneys saw me and waved.

Paul was tall and rail-thin, with brown curly hair and granny glasses. He was delightful to talk to, though I disagreed with his book-buying philosophy. Paul believed that any book was a good investment and would appreciate in value, and that the more books Susie sold on eBay, the better off they would be.

"Wow," I said. "Looks like you got the prizes."

They smiled at each other and Paul said, "New stuff mostly. But hey, there's always a market."

Susie was wearing a gray sweatshirt with a blue-and-orange New York Mets insignia, though she was originally a South Dakota girl and chubby in a wholesome, farm-raised way. Her light brown hair was scraped back in a ponytail and she blinked nearsightedly through pink-framed glasses. Her sweatshirt triggered the memory of a conversation we had had at a thrift shop in Bridgehampton recently. I'd told her about my new book appraisal job.

"Gee, why can't I find something like that? Something steady, that didn't make me feel like a gerbil in a cage? I'm already thirty-one, Delhi. The way things are, I don't know when I'll be able to have kids." She had looked at me like a doleful little girl denied birthday cake at her own party. "Paul's working at Home Depot to pay the mortgage, but he doesn't want to do that forever. He loves books, and he's better at finding good ones than I am. You either have it or you don't, I guess."

So she knew how hopeless she was. Her current life gave her no time to learn the difference between early John Updike and late Judith Krantz. Uploading book listings to eBay and mailing out sold books had to take all day and night.

Then I thought of a way that she could have the kind of income she needed and learn about books at the same time. It was a perfect solution.

"Got a minute?" I asked.

"If *you* do." Paul looked back at the ranch house that I was sure held nothing that I wanted.

"I don't know if you know it, but Marty Campagna's bought the Old Frigate. He wants to sell his books there, and maybe some paintings."

"He bought Margaret's store?"

"Well, it's a beautiful place. He doesn't want to work there himself, he only wants to use the shop as a venue. He asked me if I wanted to run it, but I was thinking that Susie would be perfect instead. It's good money."

The Pevneys exchanged a quick, surprised look.

Susie responded first. "Gee, Delhi, I don't know. I mean, Marty's up there in the stratosphere compared to us. Would he even want me touching his books?"

"Don't be silly. You're a bookseller. He's the one supplying the books for the shop anyway, not you." Realizing how condescending that sounded, I added, "He didn't offer to sell my books there either."

"But when would you list our books on eBay?" Paul asked Susie. "You've got plenty to keep you busy."

"She'd be making more money at the shop, and not have to work so hard," I told him. I didn't add that she'd be able to get on with her life.

"Yeah, but what about weekends? She couldn't work weekends, we have to go to sales."

So you can pick up crap? I'd thought that they would jump at the opportunity.

"She's got her own career to think about," Paul said loftily.

That was it? My irritation bubbled over. "Okay, fine. I thought it would be an easy eighteen dollars an hour. But I see now that it wouldn't work. Forget I said anything."

"Delhi, wait—" Susie called.

But I had already started back down the driveway. I was halfway down the street in my van before I realized who was being unreasonable. I was turning into Bianca. If people didn't do what I wanted, I wouldn't play. *Uncle Wiggily*'s owner may have honestly thought his book was worth a fortune. Paul Pevney was only responding the way I had when Marty dismissed *my* book business with a wave of his hand.

Time to give up and go home.

CHAPTER THIRTY

I WASN'T SURPRISED to find a phone message from Susie when I pressed play on my answering machine.

"Hi, Delhi! I'm sorry we acted so dumb. It was such a surprise! Paul still isn't sure, but *I* think it's a great idea. Maybe you can call me tomorrow when he's working?"

I would do that. In the meantime I had to check with Marty to make sure hiring Susie was okay with him. I didn't know if he'd be back from sales yet, so I tried him on his cell phone.

"Campagna," he barked.

"Marty? It's Delhi. I'm sorry I didn't get back to you sooner. I've been busy assessing books."

"Anything good?" He was ready to forgive me immediately for the right stuff.

"Actually, yes. It's Nate Erikson's private library. All his own books, and a lot signed to him from other writers."

"No shit! How'd you manage that?"

"Long story. But that's not why I'm calling. It's about the Old Frigate."

"And?"

"I think I have a solution. You know Susie Pevney?"

"No."

"Yes, you do. The Hoovers?"

"Oh. Yeah."

"Susie's looking for something steady, so I thought—"

"Susie Hoover? She's dumb as a stop sign."

"No, she's not!"

"You ever see the books she picks?"

"She can be taught."

"Not on my dime."

"It wouldn't only be Susie. I mean, I'd oversee things until she got settled in." A concession I had not planned on making. "She's really very organized."

"No. *You're* the one I want." His voice was as implacable as it would have been with a line crasher at a book sale.

"Think about it. I'm sure we can work something out."

He snorted and hung up.

While I was on a roll, I decided to call Marselli.

He was not in his office, but got back to me within the hour.

"Marselli. What's up?"

"Hi. I was wondering what you'd found out about Gretchen Erikson."

He seemed to be considering what he felt like telling me. "Definite asphyxiation. The signs were there from the first, cotton fibers, bloodshot eyes. She may have been drugged, but we won't know that until the tox comes back. How's the family?"

"A little cranky."

"No one acting suspiciously?" Marselli's way of making a joke.

"Did you talk to Regan Erikson?"

"The one upstate? No, but she's on the list."

"She seemed closer to Gretchen than the others. But ask her where she was when her father drowned."

"Why?"

"I don't know. There's something weird about that whole thing."

"Autopsy report, two drownings. Water in the airways. He had a contusion, consistent with striking his head on the side of the pool."

What else was there to say?

CHAPTER THIRTY-ONE

I WASN'T SURE when Marselli would interview Regan, but my phone rang Sunday afternoon. The caller ID came up as "Harada, Dai."

"Secondhand Prose!"

"Delhi?"

"Hi Regan."

"Why did you tell that policeman where I live?"

"I didn't. I don't even know where you live. Your family must have told him."

"But to come all the way up to Kinderhook—and on a Sunday morning! He even started asking me about Nate and wouldn't tell me when Gretchen's service is going to be. What an idiot."

"He probably doesn't know when. They can't plan anything until the autopsy is finished. *I'll* let you know when the service is."

"*You* will? That's another thing: For someone who's only

my sister's collaborator, you're way too chummy with the whole bunch. It's weird that you're the one who called me about my aunt. I work with lots of authors and we hardly ever see each other. You seem to be out there all the time."

"People work differently."

"I want you to tell me why! What's really going on with you?"

"What do you think is going on?"

"Don't answer my questions with questions. You know what I think? You're a con artist trying to get their money."

Lots of luck with that. "Did you want something, Regan? Or did you just call to insult me."

"No." Her voice was suddenly small. "I get carried away when I'm upset."

"I didn't sic the police on you."

Well, actually I did. I didn't say you'd done *anything though.*

"I knew they'd be a nuisance! That's why I said involving them was a mistake. They can railroad people into anything."

Was it my place to tell her that Gretchen had been suffocated? No, she had already accused me of being too involved. "They'd have to have evidence first. They don't just decide someone is guilty and go after them."

"Oh, no? You can interpret 'evidence' any way you like. Look at all those people who've been cleared by DNA years later. That detective asked Dai a lot of questions and he wouldn't even let me stay in the room."

"Maybe he wanted to get an outsider's perspective. Someone who knew the family but wasn't related."

"Dai's much too trusting. You know what he said? He told that detective that he and Gretchen didn't get along! That's all he needed to hear. It wasn't like that, Gretchen was the one who resented Dai. She did everything she could to keep us from getting married. Just because he was the gardener. Now that detective thinks Dai had a reason for hurting her."

"Regan, they know people don't always get along. If people went around killing everyone they disliked, there'd be about three of us left in the world. And why would Dai have any reason to hurt her after all these years?"

A long silence. "He wouldn't—of course he wouldn't. But innocent people go to jail with no evidence all the time." She sounded close to tears. "And he was down on Long Island when she went missing. Anyway, I've got to go, we promised the kids we'd get pumpkins. You'll keep me posted?"

I promised I would.

LATE THAT AFTERNOON I called Susie Pevney back.

"I guess you're calling about the Old Frigate?" I was dreading telling her I had offered her a job that wasn't available.

"It sounds like an answer to my prayers. Paul has some doubts, but I'm sure he'll come around."

"There are still a few details to work out," I warned.

Like holding a gun to Marty's head.

"Delhi, I'm so sick of eBay and PayPal I could take a

whip to them. By the time everyone takes their cut, I don't know why I bother. I'll work whenever he needs me to."

"I'll let you know more soon," I promised, and hoped it was a promise I could keep.

I SPENT THE rest of the afternoon in the barn, but didn't accomplish much. Some days are like that. Some days I'll pick up a book to describe and an hour later I'll still be reading it. I wished I could time travel back to the first giddy days of bookselling, back to when the economy had not yet tanked, and I could have dismissed Colin and Marty's plans for me with a laugh. Back before September, when Nate Erikson was one of my idols. I still loved his sensibility, but I was seeing him through a cloudy window. I didn't understand the destroyed painting of the young woman in the studio. I thought it was mean to give Regan money and then deny his other children what *they* needed to pursue their dreams. It was not that he owed them anything . . . except to treat them fairly. It might have been better to continue happily collecting his work without knowing anything about him.

CHAPTER THIRTY-TWO

THE POLICE WERE back at Adam's Revenge on Monday, concentrating on the area between the house and the pool, moving snaillike as they studied the ground. I wondered if they were looking for traces of someone carrying Gretchen's body down from the house. But who was strong enough? Puck and Claude could probably manage it, but not the women. Of course, two people working together could do it, Claude and Lynn or Regan and Dai. Or Bianca and Puck, though they didn't seem to like each other that much.

Then I remembered the wheelbarrow that Regan said was tipped on its side. She assumed Gretchen had tripped backward over it and fallen down into the pool. But what if Gretchen had not died in her room but in one of the cottages that was on the same level as the pool? It would have been easy for anyone to wheel her body over. The wheelbarrow had been on the terrace when Marselli first came, but there had been no reason for it to seem important.

Another thing: If Gretchen had died in her own bed, why bother moving her at all? But if she had been suffocated in Rosa's or Claude's or Bianca's cottage, there was a good reason to have her found somewhere else.

It seemed important to let the police know. I continued into the studio to leave my laptop and bag, then locked the door again and headed for the pool. I had nearly reached the opening in the cedars when a young patrolman intercepted me. He was blond with a pleasant face and lean build, the kind of face you would notice at a mall but never be able to identify afterward.

"Ma'am, this is a crime scene."

"I know—is Detective Marselli here?"

"Not yet."

"I only wanted to tell him—I guess I can tell you— that if you haven't dusted that wheelbarrow for fingerprints, you should."

"Ma'am?"

I pointed in the direction of the terrace. "It's Gretchen Erikson's wheelbarrow, the woman who died. Someone may have used it to transport her body from one of the cottages. So it should be checked out."

"Who are you?" He didn't seem to know if he should kneel down in admiration or arrest me.

"Delhi Laine. I'm the one who called the police. It's up there on the side of the hill. Or was." From where we stood I couldn't see the garden or the pool.

"Wait a minute. You're saying that the wheelbarrow's part of the crime scene? How do you know that?"

"I don't. It's just an idea. It probably doesn't mean anything. Just mention the wheelbarrow to Frank Marselli, okay?"

I knew it wouldn't make the patrolman happy, but I turned and walked away before he could ask me anything else.

CHAPTER THIRTY-THREE

BIANCA WAYLAID ME on my way back from delivering the message about the wheelbarrow. I suspected that the yellow mums she was planting in front of her chalet were an excuse to make sure she didn't miss me.

"How about some tea?" she offered.

"Okay, fine."

I went inside and sat down on the quilted floral sofa, averting my eyes from the lonely teddy bear. Bianca came back from the kitchen a minute later, carrying a tray with two beautiful Spode cups, and a matching floral sugar and creamer. Setting the tray on the coffee table in front of me, she asked, "Take anything in it?"

"No. Thanks."

"You were going to tell me why you don't take photographs anymore." She sat back in her chair, waiting, her pale eyes watching me.

"I meant to tell you before this," I said. "It's hard to talk about."

"What happened?"

"You know the photograph of the two little girls trading flowers?"

"The twins? You and your sister? No, not if you took it."

"My daughters, Hannah and Caitlin. They were twins too."

"How do you stop being—oh." Bianca didn't miss much.

I took a breath that felt ragged to me. "They were two years old when that photo was taken. We were in England for the summer at a kind of archeological institute. My daughter Jane was four, and I was pregnant with my son, Jason. I know." I smiled faintly at her look of disbelief. "It's a lot of children in a short time."

"It's what my parents were trying to do. Anyway, go on."

"Colin was off visiting a site that day and I was down by the Avon River with the girls. We went to the park every day. The story in the papers said that I was dozing on a bench, holding Hannah, when Jane came running up and told me that Caitlin had fallen in the river."

Bianca put her hand over her eyes.

"You don't have to listen to this."

"No. Go on."

"I raced down to the edge to try and find her. People heard me screaming her name and saw me thrashing around in the water and came running. The trouble was, the water was only waist-deep there but we didn't know where to look. Jane couldn't tell us where she had fallen in.

"Then that night, Jane changed her story. She was hysterical, afraid to fall asleep because she said 'the bad lady' would come and steal *her* too. We tried to get her to tell us more about this lady, but she couldn't. All she said was that she had on 'funny shoes' and promised her a bunny, then wouldn't give it to her."

I was suddenly back in that large family bedroom, holding my sweaty child, part of my mind trying to make what had happened not true, the other part fighting to understand her. That second part wanted to shake her until the truth came tumbling out of her mouth like marbles.

"Delhi, are you okay?"

I nodded and took a long sip of the peppermint-flavored tea. The English were right. Tea was bracing.

"What did the police say when you told them what she'd said?"

"We tried all night to find out more. Finally we had to let her sleep. Colin went to the station at six the next morning."

I had trouble remembering what happened after that. "They promised they would follow up. They tried to interview people who had been in the park that afternoon. People had seen us all together but no one had noticed a woman leaving with a little girl."

Another sip of tea. "I don't think they took Jane seriously. The police psychologist thought she felt guilty about not protecting Caitlin, and had invented a 'bad lady' to help her cope."

"But the details were so specific. They never found her in the water?"

"No. I think they brought in divers. But—no."

"Isn't that unusual?"

"They said it could happen, if she got caught on something. She hardly weighed anything. We borrowed money from Colin's parents to hire a private detective and I stayed on as long as I could, right up until Jason was ready to be born. We posted pictures of Caitlin everywhere. The trouble was, everyone assumed that she had drowned since that's what the police said. It's not like that other little girl who was stolen from her hotel room in Portugal, Madeleine McCann." I may have buried Caitlin and my feelings over the years, but I obsessively followed stories about missing children.

"What did your detective find?"

My throat felt too raw to talk. "Nothing," I croaked.

Bianca sighed. "What a terrible thing for your other children. Especially her twin. Something like that can scar your whole life. You never get over what might have been."

"That's what Colin thought." I took my final dose of tea. "He said that what happened to Caitlin couldn't be the thing that defined our family, to have what you called the might-have-been always looming over us. We decided the other children were young enough to let them have a normal life. Jane seemed to forget about it after it happened and Hannah and Jason never really knew."

"And your therapist agreed with that?"

"No therapist."

"You didn't *see* anyone?" She put her other hand under her teacup as if to keep from dropping it.

"We were young and only trying to survive. I guess we thought we didn't need that kind of help. We wanted to do what was best for the other kids. But now . . . I don't know." I thought about Jane in Manhattan, a financial success but changing boyfriends like Prada handbags, Hannah, my animal lover and drama queen and Jason wandering around New Mexico trying to find a way to live. Were they responding to something under the surface, a melancholy they had no idea how to define?

I remembered my conversation with Jane. "When I was talking to Jane the other night, I asked her if she could recall anything that had happened in Stratford-upon-Avon. And she said she couldn't."

"Well—" Bianca sounded skeptical.

"I know. After I asked her she started sounding weird. She got off the phone right away. I don't think she remembers anything consciously, but there's something there."

"More tea?"

"Sure. Thanks."

She set my cup on the tray and disappeared, leaving me time to gather myself for the next and harder part. I leaned back on the sofa. I wasn't sure why telling Bianca felt so good, but it was like fighting nausea for hours, pressing your lips closed and trying to think about something else, then finally giving in. You felt so much better—at least for the moment—that you wondered why you hadn't given in earlier.

When she came back with two fresh cups, she said, "What does it have to do with your not taking pictures?"

Even Colin didn't know this part. "The newspapers said I had been dozing on a park bench. Exhausted mum, too many little children, end of story. I got as much sympathy as blame." I paused, but Bianca just watched me.

"I wasn't asleep. I was busy taking photos of people in boats on the river and the girls were playing around me. I got absorbed in what I was doing and moved to the edge of the bank. I even remember what I was focusing on, two elderly women in large white hats being rowed by a young boy. Then Jane was pulling at my leg, and the rest you know."

Bianca tilted her head at me, frowning. "I don't understand. If you were that close to the river, why didn't you see her fall in? Out of the corner of your eye. Or at least heard a splash."

I stared at her. I had changed my story so quickly that no one had known to ask me that. With all the terror and confusion, some part of me had come to believe the sleeping story was true. I *was* always exhausted in those days, always nodding off in airports and poetry readings. "My God!" It came out as a wail.

"My God," she echoed.

"Of course I would have noticed. I noticed everything."

"Why did you change your story?"

"I don't know. As soon as I called him, Colin said, 'You fell asleep, didn't you? You weren't watching her because you fell asleep.' At first I told him no, but ignoring your kids to take photos seemed even worse. I knew he would never forgive that." The truth was, it was hard to remember what I had been thinking half a lifetime ago.

"So you punished yourself by giving up photography."

"I didn't think of it like that, I just wasn't interested in it anymore. I was too busy."

Bianca put her cup down as suddenly as if the steam had scalded her hand. "If you didn't see her fall in the water and nobody else did either, there's a good chance she didn't. Your daughter's story about the 'bad lady' is probably true."

I leaned forward. "You think she's *alive* somewhere?"

"Why not?"

CHAPTER THIRTY-FOUR

YET AS SOON as I left Bianca's cottage and was standing outside the studio door, doubts rushed in like a crowd of anxious shoppers once the doors have opened. I closed my eyes, trying to recall the day it happened. The park had been crowded and noisy. There was the constant drone of insects buzzing, tourists laughing and photographing each other, little shrieks from my daughters as they played. Sounds from people in boats that carried over the water. Street vendors cranking out music and ringing bells. Would I really have noticed a small splash?

Making myself remember that August day brought too much pain: Colin's despair when he realized he would never again hold his favorite child and Jane's face, all mucus and tears. Having to call my parents long distance to let them know. The blue numbness that had muffled everything so that I barely felt Jason's kicks. Before that I had known only sunshine, the certainty that each day would be a new adventure. Afterward every day brought fresh horrors.

Coming home without Caitlin was terrible but it made it easier to forget. Having three children under five was distraction enough. And so many details of those days had been lost to time. I reminded myself that the police had been satisfied, that our detective, an honorable man, had been satisfied . . .

But police in a different place and another time had also been satisfied that Nate and Morgan's deaths were accidental drownings. I was still not convinced.

I opened my eyes and stared at the green studio door, with its peeling paint. What I wanted to do most was get in my van and drive. I thought best when I was in motion, my mind just focused enough on my surroundings to keep from crashing into anything, but with an alternate commentary murmuring below the surface. Every so often an unexpected idea would splash up into consciousness like a startled trout. If I was quick, I could capture and examine it.

I was tempted to leave, but I made myself go into the studio. I would stay as long as I could bear it.

Going through Nate Erikson's fiction collection was supposed to be the icing on the cake, my reward for researching all those copies of *The Hound of the Baskervilles* and *Romeo and Juliet* in seventeen languages. I carried piles of novels to the worktable, still as shaky as a butterfly in a rainstorm. Raw life and death, the loss of a child, made books seem frivolous. But right now books were what I had.

These books didn't acquit themselves well. Many were not first editions and a few had a book club vibe. I put those that were personally inscribed to Nate or signed by the author in a separate pile.

There's a raging debate among booksellers as to which are more valuable, inscribed or just signed. Inscriptionists argue that the more of the author's handwriting there is, the better, especially if what is written is clever or revealing. Signature-only first editions have gained favor in recent years, however, as an increasing number of collectors don't want an unknown third party interfering with their experience.

Gradually the association copies worked their magic on me and calmed me down. Names like James Baldwin, William Styron, and Carson McCullers appeared like old friends. Had Nate and Eve known all of them? From the warm inscriptions, they had at least met. What was it about famous people that attracted other famous people as friends, even when they were in different spheres? They seemed to recognize that they were on similar planes of achievement and were less guarded, more receptive.

A phenomenon I could only marvel at.

AROUND FOUR THERE was a knock on the door, and Bianca came in. "I thought of something."

I smiled to encourage her to go on.

"You said you were taking pictures that day. Of people on the river—and people around you?"

"Whatever seemed interesting," I agreed.

She waited for me to understand.

It took a beat. "You think I might have photographed someone who was involved?"

"There could have been someone on the sidelines, someone who strayed into a picture, or was watching you."

I stared at her. I had last looked at the contact sheet from that day years ago, when I had printed up my last photo of Caitlin exchanging flowers with her twin. But I had not looked for anything else. Prickles of sorrow, oceans of guilt, had threatened to break through my fog back then, and I had stored those sheets quickly away. I wasn't even sure where.

Could they hold the answer to what really happened that day?

CHAPTER THIRTY-FIVE

BIANCA MET ME at my van the next morning, dressed in jeans and a white sweatshirt with a tennis club insignia. Evidently there were no committee meetings this morning.

I wasn't sure I wanted to talk about Caitlin again. I had spent the night ransacking stacks of photos and packed-away cartons, looking for the contact sheets. I couldn't find them. Had I thrown away the reminders of that afternoon in a fit of despair? I prayed not. I still had three undeveloped rolls of film as well as the negative strips, but I hadn't filed them in any order and it meant squinting at hundreds. In the end, I had fallen into bed and slept badly.

"There won't be lunch today."

"Okay."

"Mama's too upset. They've arrested Bessie." She stepped back and waited for my reaction.

I didn't disappoint her. "*What?*"

"She and Jocasta didn't come in this morning, and we

were worried. So we called. Bessie's daughter was hysterical."

"You're sure she was arrested?"

"Well, I don't think handcuffs are the latest fashion accessory. Anyway"—she eyed me reproachfully—"I thought you'd know. That your friend would have told you."

"No. I'll try to find out."

I found Frank Marselli down at the pool area, conferring with a policewoman and writing on his clipboard. He looked up when he saw me coming, then back down at what he was doing. This time the patrolman didn't try to stop me.

I went right up to him. "You've arrested Bessie?"

"Hold on. I've got things to do here."

"But why *Bessie*?"

"Over there." He pointed to the grass some distance away.

I went. I knew he didn't have to tell me anything, and he probably wouldn't. If Bessie had smothered Gretchen, he didn't even need my take on the family anymore.

He took his time talking to the others around the pool. Restless and tired of waiting, I started to walk away. This patch of grass, where Bianca had gotten sick and Claude had paced was too familiar.

Marselli saw me leaving and nodded at me to wait.

"Why are you listening to rumors?" he said impatiently when he reached me. "We brought Ms. Brown in for questioning. Period. There are a few things we need to clear up. Like why her fingerprints were in Ms. Erikson's room around the bed. We matched them and she has a prior."

"Bessie? What for?"

But he had already said more than he wanted. "It's im-
material."

"Was it for stealing?" *For having a granddaughter who
lied about her cooking skills?*

"The case was dismissed."

"Was it recent?"

"Ms. Laine." He let me see he was holding himself
in check. He would have been good at charades. "It was
something that happened over twenty years ago. And I'll
ask the questions. How did she and Gretchen Erikson get
along?"

"Fine, as far as I could see. Bessie likes everyone. They
seemed to respect each other for the jobs they did."

He nodded.

"How does she explain her fingerprints?"

I doubted he would tell me, but he said, "Claims she
sometimes helps out by changing the linen."

"That's reasonable. Are you—you know—trying to
put pressure on the family by arresting her? To make
someone else come forward?"

He stared at me from under his dark eyebrows. "I
don't play games, Ms. Laine."

I ENDED UP driving toward East Hampton for lunch, stopping at the Sea-Shell Diner. I sat on a stool at the counter
and ordered a grilled cheese sandwich and a vanilla egg
cream. *Comfort food.* Yet why was I in need of comfort?

I answered my own question. In the past two days I had

torn open my construction-paper life, and burrowed frantically through old cartons to find something that probably didn't exist anymore. Now there was the news that Bessie had been arrested. The only thing I could imagine that would drive Bessie to hurt someone was if Gretchen had physically attacked Eve. Even then she would have done nothing more than pull them apart. It made an incongruous picture, the three women in a fistfight.

As soon as I had decided that, though, a possibility crossed my mind, faint as a curtain ruffling in a summer breeze. What if Gretchen had discovered proof that Eve had been responsible for Nate's death? Suppose she had been planning to reveal it at the memorial but Eve and Bessie had silenced her instead? Eve could have given her a sedative during their afternoon tea, making it easier to smother her, and Bessie could have moved her to the pool in the cover of night.

Of course, I knew no reason that Eve would have to hurt Nate or, even less likely Morgan. True, she hadn't rushed to her defense when Puck attacked her, but that didn't mean she wished her granddaughter harm.

I picked at the coleslaw in the pleated paper cup and tried to imagine why Bessie would have been arrested years ago. Maybe she had been desperate for money and had written bad checks. Or been caught driving without insurance. Nothing like murder.

Marselli claimed he wasn't playing games. But I wondered.

CHAPTER THIRTY-SIX

WHEN I GOT back to the Eriksons, Bianca was standing in the gravel circle, arms crossed like a teacher waiting for a playground straggler. *Now what?*

"We're having a family meeting. Where have you been?"

What had happened to yesterday's closeness? "I was hungry. I wanted lunch. And I'm not part of your family."

"Well, they want you there."

"Is the meeting about Bessie?" I reminded myself that I was an adult, that I didn't have to take their abuse for Eve's aide getting arrested. Then I remembered Marselli, and how we both wanted to find out the truth, and followed Bianca into the house.

The family was once again sitting in the great room. I half expected to see Regan there too, scowling at me. Lynn and Claude sat as motionless as a Grant Wood painting in the center of one couch, but he had his arm around her

and her head was on his shoulder. Eve and Rosa, more relaxed on a sofa opposite, had nonetheless left the space of
a cushion between them, an eerie reminder of Gretchen's
empty seat at the memorial.

Puck had settled himself in the same striped wing
chair he'd sat in the day we had lunch here, but today he
had turned it away from the window and was facing into
the room. He grinned at me when I came in, but I had
learned not to trust his good humor.

Two Windsor chairs had been brought in from the
dining room and forced into the circle. I sat down in one
of them.

Miss Scarlet in the conservatory under attack.

Claude cleared his throat. "Puck's found out some interesting things about Bessie."

He nodded to his brother, ceding him the floor.

Puck gave us his impish look, fair eyebrows raised. "It
seems our Bessie has been tripped up by the law before."

Bianca, beside me, drew in a breath, but Eve remained
impassive.

"You said that. But you never told Claude why," Lynn
said.

Puck tilted his curly head. "Bessie's been a home health
aide on Long Island for years. In 1991 she was caring for
a young woman in Shoreham, a woman who was in a lot
of pain and kept telling everybody she wanted to die. And
then, one day, she did."

"Was she terminal?" It wasn't my place to speak up,
but the way the others were nodding in comprehension
was too irritating to let pass.

"Yes, but that's not what she died from. The coroner said she had been suffocated." He emphasized the last word, looking as pleased as if he had baffled us with a magic trick.

That did give me a jolt. I wasn't sure if the others knew how Gretchen had died, so they might not pick up the connection. But what were the odds of two women dying the same way when Bessie was close by?

"Did they put her in jail?" Rosa asked, alarmed.

"'Ay, there's the rub.' Evidently the young woman was facedown in bed when they found her, with no sign of any marks. So she could have pressed her face into the pillow herself. There were other discrepancies, and in the end the DA decided not to prosecute. The case was dropped. No conviction, no jail."

"What was wrong with the young woman?" Lynn asked softly.

Puck looked at her as if she had missed the point. "I don't know, ALS I think, that Lou Gehrig disease. She wasn't completely paralyzed yet, she could still talk."

I forced myself to keep quiet.

"But Gretchen wasn't a candidate for mercy killing," Bianca said. "She wasn't asking to die."

"Well duh, Bianca. When you've killed once, it's easy to kill again."

And you know that because? "What's her motive? You still have to have a motive." If they wanted me there they were going to get me.

"There's something else." Claude leaned forward. "Mama, do you want to tell them?"

Eve's eyes flicked over the group, then she gave her head a shake.

"Late Saturday night, when we were getting ready for the memorial, Mama opened her bedroom door to use the bathroom. At the end of the hall she saw Bessie carrying something, going down the stairs. Isn't that what you told me, Mama?"

Eve gave a weary nod.

"Mama thought it was laundry. But I think it must have been Gretchen."

I felt stunned. "What did the police think?"

"That's why we're telling *you*. So you can tell your friend. We don't want Mama being cross-examined by the police."

I opened my mouth to say that the police would have to question her about something so important, then closed it again. That was Marselli's problem, not mine.

"Poor Bessie," said Rosa sadly. "I liked Bessie."

"Bessie?" Bianca looked ready to jump up and shake Rosa. "Bessie killed Gretchen. She's not 'Poor Bessie.'"

"But what reason could she have?" I said.

"People do crazy things. Maybe Gretchen threatened to get her fired—you hear about disgruntled employees all the time, coming back and killing people. Maybe she wanted Jocasta to get the job cooking."

"That would be crazy," I agreed.

"People lose control and go berserk." Lynn spoke as one who knew. "And Bessie's very strong. She has to be to lift people in and out of wheelchairs."

"I'm sure the police will find out what was behind it."

Claude swept away my question of motive with an airy hand.

"While we're having a family meeting I want to say something," Bianca broke in, cheeks flushing pink. "Rosa, you have to clean your place up, it's getting worse and worse. It's a disgrace for people who come here to have to look at."

Rosa jerked up on the sofa as though she had been slapped. "No, it isn't."

"Didn't you say some of the things were Gretchen's anyway?" Lynn asked.

"Yes, and I'm not giving them up."

"But they don't belong to you," Claude said severely, as he would to a child who had taken someone else's toy. "What are these things, anyway?"

"I'm not telling." Rosa hunched back down into the sofa, arms crossed.

Puck held up a hand to silence Claude, then said to Rosa, "Bigger than a bread box?"

"What?"

"Remember twenty questions? You have to answer yes or no."

Her eyes flickered around the room for confirmation.

"Is it bigger than a chair? Or little, like a piece of paper," he coaxed.

"Yes."

"You mean there's lots of things. A chair *and* some papers."

She smiled, understanding what was expected of her. "Not a *chair*."

"A table?"

"No!"

"Important papers?"

This was excruciating—and dangerous. "If you want me to talk to Marselli, I have to go," I interrupted. "Rosa, come on. I have something to give you."

She got up eagerly. I didn't look at anyone as we left.

CHAPTER THIRTY-SEVEN

CLAUDE CAUGHT UP with us on the front steps. I expected him to order Rosa back inside, but he said to me, "You'll tell the police what Mama saw?"

"I said I would."

"How much longer for the books?"

"Only a few days." Was I glad or sorry? I'd gotten used to driving out to Springs every morning and not having to worry about money. On the other hand, negotiating my way through this family had been an emotional obstacle course.

"Are the books worth anything?"

I hated hearing him refer to them as commodities, but I said, "Of course. It's a good thing you didn't put them out when you had that book sale."

He chuckled. "That was an audition—to find the right appraiser. We didn't want anyone who looked too professional, who would raise Mama's suspicions. We needed someone competent, but who looked like she could be Bianca's collaborator."

One mystery solved.

He kept pace with me. Rosa did too on the other side, eager for what I had promised her. "What do we owe you? I know it's been a while since I wrote you a check."

It had been less than a week, but I wasn't going to refuse the money. "I'm not sure."

"Don't worry, I'll figure the total out. Stop by the house on your way home." He gave my arm a pat, then turned back to the house.

I racked my brain for something I could offer Rosa. "I have some Beanie Babies at home. I'll bring them tomorrow."

"I love those!"

"In the meantime, don't tell anyone about anything Gretchen gave you. That was right that you didn't." I thought of something else. "There used to be a girl who came here with hair like mine."

"Sonia?"

"Do you know her last name?"

"No one said her name. She loved my father too, but she went away."

I realized I was holding my breath. "Do you know why?"

"She got hurt."

We had started down the hill in the direction of where Marselli was working. I breathed out. "How did she get hurt?"

But Rosa saw her cottage. "I have to make more plates now," she said urgently, and broke into a clumsy run.

If it had been someone else, I might have been startled. But I was beginning to understand how Rosa's mind worked.

I was relieved to see that the area around the pool was deserted. It would give me more time to think before I told Marselli anything. I hated to give him more damning information about Bessie. Although she seemed devoted to Eve Erikson, I sensed that she had deeper loyalties, claims of family and community, and that in the end her connection to the Eriksons was as a job. I doubted she would let herself be drawn so deeply into a family drama not her own.

Yet that was only my sense. Eve's claim to have seen Bessie carrying something heavy down the stairs was particularly damning because of the affection between them. Yet how reliable was Eve? *She* hadn't said it was Gretchen. If it was before the memorial, Bessie was probably on her way home, carrying her own things. A body might be Claude's wishful thinking. Eve might have mentioned seeing Bessie leaving that night, and he had jumped on it like powdered sugar on donuts.

AT FIVE-THIRTY I walked over to Claude and Lynn's. Although their house had been built to resemble a one-room schoolhouse, complete with a brass bell in a cupola, there were two stories and obviously more rooms.

I was expecting him to appear at the door, checkbook in hand, but Lynn was the one who opened it. "Delhi! Is everything okay?"

"Claude asked me to stop by for a check."

"Oh—come in." She pulled back the door.

The house had the charm that comes from the simplicity of colonial antiques and bare wooden floors. A well-placed stoneware pitcher, white ruffled curtains, apples and oranges in bowls. Rocking chairs by the fireplace and a basket of wood. The black wrought-iron candlesticks were a reminder that there had not always been electricity.

A perfect period piece.

I noticed a large quilt hanging on the wall, vibrant in reds and greens.

"That's gorgeous!"

"Thank you. It's a Double Wedding Ring. I made all the quilts in the house."

"Wow. *Everyone* in this family is creative."

She brushed back a wing of blond hair. "Creative? Not in Nate and Eve's book. They thought they were the opposite of 'creative.' My sin was to use traditional patterns instead of making up my own."

"But the colors are wonderful."

"They are, but you know what? They were right. A few years ago I saw an exhibit of quilts from Gee's Bend, this very poor black community in Alabama. They used whatever old cloth they could spare and made up their own patterns. I was blown away. Now I make my own designs too, reflecting the seasons and the sea. Slow, but I'm getting there."

"Good for you. By the way, I liked your toast to Gretchen. I was glad someone remembered her."

"Poor Gretchen. I hope they don't put *her* in the urn, too. That whole thing creeps me out. People belong in cemeteries, not on the dining room table."

"It is unusual."

"Nate would have thought it was ridiculous. Everything made more sense when he was alive. Without him you can see the cracks."

"What cracks? Where?" Claude appeared from the hall. To my surprise, he was cradling a small black puppy. "Meet Jellybean." He planted a soft kiss on the dog's fuzzy head. "She keeps us hopping."

"Not a Shakespearean name."

"No, she's a little devil."

"I didn't know anyone had pets here."

"Nate wouldn't allow animals," Lynn explained. "He had a bad experience growing up. But now we have this little cutie." She reached over and nuzzled the dog too.

Jellybean squirmed as if trying to reach Lynn, and Claude handed her to his wife. Then he reached into a maroon dressing gown pocket and handed me an envelope. "I made it for the same amount as last time. Is that okay?"

"That's fine, but—"

"What did the police say?"

"The police? Oh—they'd already left. I'll call Detective Marselli as soon as I get home."

He looked as disappointed as if I had muffed a save for his favorite team.

"You know," I said to Lynn, "you mentioned that Gretchen was taking care of Morgan that morning. Where was the au pair, Sonia?"

Claude's face told me I was off the team completely. Lynn looked defensive. "It was only for that week, after Sonia was . . ." Her voice trailed away.

"Your biggest mistake was bringing her here," Claude snapped at her.

"*My* biggest mistake? Your family was the one who ground her up in little pieces."

"No, she was the one who—" He remembered I was still there. "We'll see you Monday." He opened the door and waited for me to leave.

I lingered on the porch for a minute but I couldn't hear anything. Sonia had gotten hurt at the compound and no one wanted to talk about it. Where was she now? Had she *died*?

I started up the hill toward my van. Getting tangled up with this family was not healthy. Not for Gretchen, not for Bessie, and evidently not for Sonia. Would I be their next casualty?

CHAPTER THIRTY-EIGHT

I PULLED OVER on Montauk Highway to phone Marselli and reached him at his desk in Hauppauge.

"I have a message for you from the family."

"Let me guess. They're best friends with the governor, and I'll be hearing from their attorney."

"They know about Bessie's past."

"Damn Internet."

"That's not what they want me to tell you. Eve says she saw Bessie going down the stairs Saturday night, carrying something. Presumably someone."

"Eve is the mother?"

"Uh-huh. Bessie's her personal attendant. The family wanted me to pass the information on to you so you don't question Mama and upset her."

"What's wrong with her, anyway?"

"Nothing physical that I can see. Sometimes she doesn't seem to be quite with it, she drifts into other time periods.

But *I* think she's pretty sharp. My feeling is, she's always been a little eccentric and her husband's death only made it worse. He took their way of life with him to the grave."

"How poetic. But she knows who Bessie is?"

"Of course she knows who Bessie is! She knows who I am. I think the family sees it as worse than it is, but it gets her a lot of attention. Everyone's afraid of crossing her. Anyway, what's Bessie's motive? I can't think of any motive."

"You've been reading too many mystery novels, Ms. Laine."

And he clicked off.

I put my phone away and drove home. As soon as I walked through the kitchen door, I was overtaken by the past. I didn't have many memories of Caitlin here, but this was the home we had come back to without her. Going over to the harvest gold electric range, I heated up a can of chili, then sprinkled low-fat cheddar over it and spooned sour cream on top. Since it was red meat, I poured a glass of Cabernet. Then I carried everything out to the computer in the barn.

Once there, I didn't know how to start searching. Even if Caitlin hadn't drowned, even if someone had taken her, how would we ever find her? What if it had been a spontaneous act, someone who saw me pregnant and struggling with three little children, and decided that one of them deserved a better life? If her abductors had never told her she was adopted . . . why would they? When you kidnapped a toddler you probably didn't bother with the niceties. Would she remember anything about her first family at all?

Her first family. Not only me, but an identical twin, a father, a brother, another sister. Five of us, yet her father seemed to have laid her to rest emotionally and the other children couldn't remember her. How much would Caitlin and Hannah still look alike? How long would it take to look at every picture posted on Facebook, even if that were allowed? The Internet had its limitations. I couldn't think of a way to search for someone without a name or correct date of birth, someone living in another country. We could perhaps post a photo of Hannah and ask anyone who knew someone who looked like her to get in touch with us. *The Hannah Fitzhugh Look-Alike Contest.*

But to do that I would have to tell Hannah that she had a twin and deal with the fallout. I would have to discuss what we should do with the whole family. Was it fair to rip away the scab that had formed over the past, and expose something that might not even be true?

Sleep on it, my father had always counseled. But I would need more than one night to decide something this important.

CHAPTER THIRTY-NINE

WHEN I WOKE up the next morning, I didn't feel like driving out to Springs. I was tired of the Eriksons and their on-again-off-again treatment of me. As long as you said what they wanted to hear, you were their friend. If you didn't, you were as welcome as a plate of cold French fries. It was hard to believe that only two weeks ago I had been thrilled about seeing Nate Erikson's library and meeting his family.

On the other hand, if I could finish up the association copies and any other books I had overlooked, I would never have to set foot on Cooper's Farm Lane again. Even if I had to work through lunch and stay late tonight, it would be worth it to get on with my life.

Nate Erikson was still my hero but, as Lynn had pointed out, paradise had a few cracks.

Remembering my promise to Rosa, I went into the eaves of the house and picked out a handful of Beanie

Babies that I was sure the girls would never miss. Then at Qwikjava I bought a tuna salad wrap and a bottle of water.

The most detailed plans are the ones that get ripped up first.

As soon as I pulled onto the gravel driveway, and saw two blue-and-white police cars and a red fire chief's sedan, my discontent flamed into dread. What had happened *now*? This time I didn't think about the books. Two police cars wouldn't be here for a fire in an empty studio. When I opened the van door and stepped down there was a smell of cinders in the air, an eerie reminder of the incinerated photograph.

As I started down the hill, I saw that Bianca's cottage, at least, had been spared. Then I was distracted by motion to my left. I turned and stared at the blackened hulk of what had once been Rosa's chalet. My first thought, *She won't be able to survive losing her stuff*, was replaced by *My God, I hope she wasn't inside!* And then the odd idea: *What if it had been a mass cremation—the only way Rosa could make herself part with her things?*

Frank Marselli's car hadn't been parked in the circle, so I wasn't going to venture over to the fire scene and draw attention to myself. Instead, I went to Bianca's chalet. The yellow rockers, still standing at attention on the tiny porch, had been joined by two pots of orange chrysanthemums and several pumpkins. It made the kind of pretty picture you would see on a New England calendar.

I knocked on the black door. No one answered and I could not hear Bianca moving around inside.

She must be up at the main house. I knew she ate breakfast there with the family, but she was usually done by the time I arrived.

Did I have the nerve to go up to the house, especially if the news was grim? Was it less daunting to throw myself into a nest of unfamiliar policemen? I *had* to know what had happened to Rosa.

I chose the policemen.

When I was nearly at the remains of the cottage, the odor of ashes already stinging my nostrils, Marselli stepped around the side of the house.

"I was wondering when you'd get here." It was not a complaint, not exactly, but more than a statement of fact.

"I didn't see your car."

But I was too caught up in what I was seeing to hear what he answered. The fire had blackened the pink-cheeked faces of Snow White and her entourage, and the metal of the outdoor grills and lawn furniture been twisted into strange shapes. Saddest of all, the stack of hopeful Easter baskets had completely disappeared. "It must have burned hot."

He nodded. "Chemical fire. The worst."

"Well, she had a lot of solvents."

"Where'd she keep them?"

"In the back of the cottage. In the kitchen area."

He looked moody. "That's not where the fire started. Not the only place. Someone made sure it would go up all at once."

Though I'd known it was possible, I felt sucker-punched. "Rosa was inside?"

"Oh, yeah. Four in the morning?" He watched my reaction, then said, "But someone dragged her out to the grass."

"Is she *okay*? How do you know she didn't stagger out herself?"

"They found her unconscious, but not from smoke inhalation. Either someone hit her on the back of the head or banged it getting her outside. Don't worry, we're keeping a watch in the hospital."

"Could she have started the fire herself?"

He cocked his head. "Why would you say that?"

Because part of me wondered if Rosa was the one who had attacked and drowned Nate and Morgan. Maybe Gretchen had seen something, but was keeping quiet until she could announce what it was at the memorial. So Rosa had had to smother her, and was overcome by remorse. She couldn't leave her things behind at the mercy of her family.

"Why would you say that?" he repeated. "Was she depressed?"

"No. But she always seemed—I don't know—off-balance. Every time she said something people jumped all over her. It's probably why she never said much. She'd suffered some brain damage from an accident as a child."

Marselli's hazel eyes flicked back to the hulking ruin. "Gives new meaning to the word 'firetrap.' The firemen couldn't even get inside."

"Someone called the fire department?"

"A woman. I don't know who yet."

"Maybe it was the person who set the fire and left Rosa

outside. They wouldn't have wanted the fire to spread to the other buildings."

He looked thoughtful at that: "You going to be around?"

"In the studio. Today was supposed to be my last day." It came out sounding plaintive. It was hard to imagine concentrating on the books now enough to finish up.

And then I thought of the thing that should have leapt to mind immediately.

CHAPTER FORTY

You have to hide this for me. But you can't read it unless something bad happens to me.

I went back to the van to retrieve Rosa's envelope to give to the police. Thank God I hadn't left it in my house.

Slipping behind the steering wheel, I leaned over and opened the glove compartment, then sat for a moment with the white envelope in my hand. Was I holding a confession to murder? Did it implicate someone else, someone who assumed the envelope had been in Rosa's cottage?

I had to know. After all, she had given me the envelope with the understanding that I should read it and act on it if anything happened to her. If I handed it to Marselli without knowing what was inside, he might never tell me what it said. Rosa was unconscious, but safe. A delay of a minute or two couldn't matter.

Yet I couldn't open the envelope sitting in the drive-way. I couldn't risk someone slipping out of the house and coming up behind me to see what I was reading, or have Marselli remembering something he wanted to ask me and sauntering over.

My heart banging, I started the engine. Bianca might think I was leaving for the day, but I didn't care.

Once out on Cooper's Farm Lane, I wasn't even sure where I was headed. At first I planned to park just out of sight, then turned left onto Springs–Fireplace Road and started to drive. When I saw the Pollock-Krasner homestead I veered into the parking lot. There were already about fifteen cars outside the gray-shingled house. Having other people around, visitors and volunteers, made me feel safer.

As I slit the envelope open with my car key, trying to do as little damage as possible, I thought again that I should have turned it over to Marselli, unread. *But you were the one she gave it to. You don't know that it has anything to do with Gretchen's murder or the cottage burning down.*

On the other hand, how could it not?

And then it was too late, I was already unfolding the two-page document. I was looking at the last will and testament of Gretchen Elspeth Erikson.

From my frisson of disappointment, I realized I had been expecting something dramatic: an indictment of the twisted darkness of the Eriksons, or a confession from Rosa as to the other deaths. What did Gretchen have to bequeath except her garden tools and a sentimental brooch or two? Rosa probably thought that any will was important.

I kept reading. Gretchen had had a formal will drawn up because she had over two million dollars in bank accounts and various funds. There were references to stock portfolios as well. The bulk of her estate had been left to "my beloved daughter," Regan Erikson. But Claude, Bianca, Puck, and Rosa had each been left $250,000 to "follow where their dreams take them." The only other beneficiary named was Peter, Claude and Lynn's son, with the stipulation that he use the money to travel around the world.

My beloved daughter, Regan Erikson. Not only had I not known, I hadn't even guessed. There had been a few hints of course: Regan so concerned that Gretchen hadn't been at the memorial, her deep shock at finding Gretchen's body. The fact that Regan bore no physical resemblance to Eve and had felt able to insult her so casually. But if Gretchen was her mother, Nate was surely not her father. *Was he?*

The will changed my perception of everything. Was this what someone had ransacked Gretchen's room looking for? Rosa must have sensed the danger when she gave me the envelope. Why else would she have been worried that something was going to happen to her? Rather than try and find the will in all that clutter, someone had decided it would be easier to destroy everything.

But why would anyone want to *destroy* the will? Everyone benefited. Had they known about it? If there were no will, then Gretchen would be considered to have died intestate and an administrator would be appointed. The proceeds would eventually be distributed among Gretchen's closest relatives—in this case, her nieces and nephews, all of them sharing equally. They would finally have the money to get on with their lives.

There was an even faster way. If Gretchen's checkbook had been taken from her room, "bequests" could be made right away. Risky, but another reason to keep her death a secret until the checks had cleared. If the bank didn't know when she died, it would be harder to prove she had not written the checks herself. Claude was skilled in signing his mother's name—why not Gretchen's?

Had Regan and Dai known how much she was going to inherit?

There was another paper in the envelope.

A car pulled up beside me, and I jumped, knocking everything off my lap. When I looked over, a young couple was climbing out of a blue Toyota. Their dreamy expressions told me that Jackson Pollock was still making conquests. I watched them scramble up the white porch steps, hand-in-hand.

The paper was crinkled, the ink washed out in some places, reminding me of a spelling test of Jason's that had gone through the laundry. The handwriting appeared to be a woman's, but the few legible words did not tell me anything. *love you and . . . a new life . . . forget what. . .*

I needed to get this will and the waterlogged paper to Marselli fast.

HE WAS STILL down at Rosa's cottage.

"I need to talk to you."

"Not now, Ms. Laine."

"No, it's important. I have to give you something Rosa gave me to keep for her."

"What is it?" He finally gave me his attention.

I looked over at the black hulk of the chalet, at the technician taking samples from its base, at the other cops studying the grounds farther away. Handing the will over to him here would be safe enough. No one would come up and snatch the pages from his hand. But anyone in the family looking out the window would be able to see me hand him something white, see him read it, and have a good idea what it was.

"Can we talk in the studio?"

"Why?" He seemed to root himself more firmly into the grass.

"I think it may be the reason why Gretchen died."

"Okay." He reached over, took my arm, and turned me around. He didn't say, *This better be good*, but the thought hovered in the smoky air.

"TELL ME AGAIN when you got this." Frank Marselli was making a point.

"Last Wednesday."

"And you opened this when?"

"Just now. It was addressed to *me*." Okay, not addressed to, but given to me.

"It didn't occur to you that if you had turned this over to the police, this young woman might not be in the hospital fighting for her life?"

"No! She specifically told me *not* to open it. She made

me promise. She said that something bad would happen to me if I did."

"So you couldn't have given me the envelope un-opened."

"I didn't know it had anything to do with Gretchen."

His hazel eyes said, *Oh, please.*

We had been down this road before.

"I'm sorry," I said. I wasn't. But I wasn't as cavalier as I sounded. Why *hadn't* I thought of turning the envelope over to Marselli last week? Yes, I had promised Rosa, but once Gretchen had been found . . . "I guess I thought she was being melodramatic. At the time."

"What's this other thing?"

"It was like that when I found it. I didn't—"

We froze as we heard a click and the studio door opened.

CHAPTER FORTY-ONE

"I KNEW I'D find you here," Bianca said tersely. Her ginger
hair framed her face in tangled bursts and she had no
makeup on. I had never noticed before how many freckles she had. For the first time I realized that if she hadn't
been Nate Erikson's daughter, she would have looked like
anyone. The waitress at the Ground Round, a stewardess
on Aer Lingus.

"I saw your van, but I didn't think it would be business as usual with you."

So she was going to play it that way. Perhaps she
wanted to show Marselli what a concerned sister she was.

I felt a familiar red tide creeping up the back of my
neck. "Where did you expect me to be? I stopped at your
cottage but no one was there."

"I was up at the house. It's not rocket science to figure
that out."

Come on, Bianca. You didn't even like Rosa.

"Terrible things are happening and all you can think about are books. You came down here to work just as if nothing had happened."

I hadn't, of course, but I couldn't tell her what I had been doing instead. I turned to Marselli, who was observing us, interested.

"Your family hasn't been very cordial to me the last few days. Why would I intrude on them when they're upset about Rosa and the fire?"

She shook her head. "I'll never understand you."

Back at ya. But it was time to stop this. "I'm worried about Rosa too. I hope she'll be okay."

"It's not as if we didn't warn her."

"You warned her?" Now Marselli couldn't resist.

"About her stuff! That cottage was a fire waiting to happen. If only she'd listened to us and cleaned things out, she wouldn't be in the hospital now. She could have destroyed the whole compound!"

Didn't Bianca know that the fire had been deliberately set? "You haven't talked to the family?" I asked Marselli.

Bianca shook her head. "At least they had the courtesy not to intrude on our grief."

They get credit for that and I don't?

"I'll see you at lunch." She turned to move away.

"Well—okay." I could always have my tuna wrap for dinner. "Is Jocasta cooking?"

She turned on me. "Of course not! Without Bessie, she didn't have a ride. I don't think the family wants a reminder of what happened to Gretchen anyway."

"I guess not."

As soon as Bianca had snapped the door closed behind her, I said, "But Bessie couldn't have set the fire—you're still holding her."

He squinted at me.

"Aren't you?"

"We brought her in for questioning. That was all."

"You mean you let her go? She's home?"

"Not for long."

"But—she'd have no reason to attack Rosa. No motive."

Marselli sighed. "What is it with you people? You seem to think that we have can't arrest anyone till we know *why* they did something. The evidence is what counts."

"Believe me, it wasn't Bessie."

"And you know that because?"

"I think that people have to have a good reason for killing someone."

"I'm sure she does. We just don't know what it is yet."

"It doesn't seem fair that the people with the least resources are always the first to be blamed."

He shrugged. "Facts are facts. The family doesn't understand how Bessie's fingerprints got around Gretchen's bed. They said she *never* did laundry."

"They're lying. They're trying to throw her under the bus to save themselves."

Marselli smiled.

CHAPTER FORTY-TWO

WHEN MARSELLI LEFT I sat on Nate Erikson's metal stool, thinking about Rosa.

I had not gotten very far when the door clicked and I jumped, knocking over my empty coffee cup. I assumed that Bianca had come back to apologize, but someone I didn't recognize at first stepped inside. Regan looked like a 1940s cigarette ad in her houndstooth-checked suit and jaunty matching hat with a feather. Even her peaked red lips were retro. Again I wondered where she bought her clothes.

"Working on your illustrations?" she asked.

"No. Just thinking about the fire."

"Can you believe it? It's one terrible thing here after another. They say bad things happen in threes, and this is already four! I came down yesterday to bring some work to two galleries. I was about to go home when Bianca called. She'd gotten my cell number from Dai and thought I should know."

I wondered why Regan felt she had to explain it to me.

She came over and leaned against the worktable. "And to have it happen to Rosa. She was always such a lost soul, trying to fit in. She was like a puppy dog around Nate. Pathetic."

"How long are you staying? Are you invited to lunch?"

"Oh, God. The Family Gathering." She rolled her eyes. "I can't believe that's still going on. Of course I'm not invited. I have to stick around to talk to that detective. I think he's punishing me by making me wait." She stood up, but left her black purse on the worktable. "I've never had a chance to look around here. Everything was always so hush-hush." She headed for the bins of paintings.

"There's a painting in there I don't understand."

She turned with an ironic smile. "Only one?"

"It's not one of the illustrations." I went over to where I remembered pushing the slashed nude back into place, then felt around until I found it. This time I was careful not to let the canvas get snagged on anything.

"My God." She took the canvas, holding it away from her to get a better look.

"Do you know who she is?"

"No. After my time, but she sure pissed someone off."

"Ya think?"

Dark humor.

"The paint's still fresh. Acrylic gets dusty after a while. Nate painted it though."

"Didn't he paint everything?"

She looked at me consideringly.

"Do you think he was involved with her and it ended badly?" I asked.

"Could be. The thing is, Nate was not usually a womanizer. Or if he was, he kept it well-hidden." She looked over at the collection of costumes. "You know what? Being in here creeps me out. Let's go for a walk or something."

I looked at her perky suit and heels.

"I have other clothes in the car. I'll change. Meet me in five minutes." She moved back to the table and picked up her purse.

"Okay." I didn't remind her to tell Marselli that she was leaving. I was no one's keeper but my own.

WHEN I REACHED the parking area I found Regan behind the wheel of a white SUV, now wearing jeans and a paint-streaked sweatshirt. She had pulled her dark hair into a ponytail.

Backing out of the driveway, she said, "It seems like there were years when we never left the property, but that can't be true, can it? We didn't go to school, but we weren't *that* isolated. Still, when you live out here, you don't run down to the local 7-Eleven for milk. I thought once everyone grew up they'd be glad to leave, but no one did. It was too much like the Magic Kingdom, I guess."

"Where would they have gone?"

She turned right on Springs–Fireplace Road. "It's a big world out there, Ms. Bookseller."

I laughed. "Nate's not your father, is he?" Not if Gretchen was your mother and you were born after Bianca and Claude. *My beloved daughter, Regan . . .*

She swerved, then straightened the wheel. "Who told you that? I didn't know anyone else knew that."

"Nobody told me. It's just the way you talk about him. You call him Nate, not Dad like everyone else."

She nodded. "He isn't my real father, but I was raised to think he was." She turned onto a road bumpy with beach grass and sand. "A few years ago I found out that Gretchen came here just before I was born. She was old enough to know better, but she'd met someone at an artist colony. Anyway, her family had taken Nate in when *he* had no one. She and Nate were close and he was happy to raise me as one of his kids."

"You never knew?"

"Never. It all came bursting out when I wanted to leave. Dai and I asked him for help, for money, and he refused. Eve told me I wasn't even their child. What a bitch she is. Gretchen was the one who gave us the money and explained everything. I always knew she loved me, certainly more than Eve did. But I loved her like my *aunt*. I can't explain, but even when she told me, I couldn't change my feelings just like that." She parked at the end of the road beside a narrow strip of beach. The bay stretched beyond us like a table waiting to be set.

"She never thought about taking you and leaving when you were older?"

"Why should she?" She opened her door. "You know what? You ask a lot of questions."

We walked over to the strip of sand which, up close, wasn't really sand, but tiny rocks. The water lapped tentatively against them as if not sure of its welcome. It was hard to imagine anyone coming here to swim with all the beautiful ocean beaches of the Hamptons. We were the only people here today, the salt air fresh on our faces.

"We used to have picnics here and pretend we were explorers looking across at China. *We* should have stopped today and gotten a picnic."

"That's okay. I'm supposed to have lunch with your family. Or was."

She found a low boulder and sat down. "They'll survive."

I knelt on the sand beside her, trying to get comfortable. "You looked as if you wanted to say something back in the studio."

"I did?"

"When I said didn't Nate paint everything?"

"You saw my father's—Nate's—paintings at the memorial. What did you think of them?"

"They were impressionistic." *And not that good.* "Different from his book illustrations."

"He came back from Vietnam with something wrong with his eyes. Not that bad at first, but it kept getting worse."

I remembered the powerful magnifying glasses on the worktable. "How terrible! What did he do?"

"Do about what?"

"If he couldn't see to paint."

"Oh. He worked it out." She pushed herself up.

"How?"

She made a noise that was close to a laugh. "Stop with the questions already. I should be asking you some. Like why you're out here all the time. Why you're so interested in my family."

"I told you. Bianca and I—"

"I don't believe that for one minute." She started back toward the parking lot and I trailed her. "You know what I think?"

I waited for her to again accuse me of trying to cheat the family out of their money. Or maybe she thought I was a cougar on the prowl, hoping to ensnare Puck. *Lots of luck with that too.*

"You're a journalist. You're writing a book about my family. You're trying to find out as much as you can to put in your exposé—and I've already told you much too much." She banged her fist against her temple theatrically. "Stupid, stupid, stupid!"

It was so far from what I was expecting, that I began to laugh. "The truth is much more boring."

"I don't believe you. Try me."

"Your family hired me to appraise your father—Nate's books, and let them know how much they're worth. It's a big secret because Eve isn't supposed to know."

"That's it?"

"That's it."

She pulled the SUV door open. "I like my story better. I'm always trying to make people more interesting than they are."

Had I just been insulted?

CHAPTER FORTY-THREE

WHEN WE PULLED onto the gravel area back at Adam's Revenge, Bianca was waiting for us.

"I kidnapped Delhi for lunch," Regan told her cheerfully. "It felt too creepy around here."

"You could have had lunch with us."

"*Really*."

"We're still a family. Now more than ever."

"How was lunch?" I asked Bianca.

"Terrible. Right before we sat down your detective came up to the house and said that someone set Rosa's cottage on fire on purpose. He thinks it was one of us! How can that be? Bessie is in jail, but Claude thinks she sent Jocasta over to start the fire."

"I thought Jocasta didn't have a car."

"Ask the police." She turned toward the house and left.

"See what I had to put up with all these years?" Regan said.

She went off to find Marselli and I went down to the studio just long enough to pack up my computer, my thermal coffee cup, and my tuna salad wrap. Then I left for the day. As I backed up my van on the gravel, the significance of what Bianca had said registered. The family was upset at lunch, not because Rosa had almost burned to death, but because suspicion might be cast on one of them.

Three deaths and six people who might be responsible, eight if you counted Regan and Dai. Yet it was hard to shake my belief that Rosa had been involved in the first three deaths, then saw suicide as the only way out. If that envelope had only contained a confession instead of Gretchen's will and the other fragment . . .

Once I was driving toward East Hampton, steering with one hand and eating my sandwich with the other, I thought of something else. What if everything had started with an even earlier death? I still didn't know what had happened to Sonia. How had Lynn put it? *Ground up in little pieces by your family.* Could Sonia have been Rosa's first victim? There was another possibility as well, but that scenario was even murkier, as obscured as Gretchen's face had been in the swimming pool.

Finding out what had happened to Sonia seemed to be the next step.

If someone didn't find out the truth, Bessie would take the blame and this time go to trial. Marselli had great integrity, but no imagination. He had no patience with nuance, of catching the faintest scent and trying to track down what it meant. Now that he had Bessie's fingerprints and an eyewitness who saw her carrying something bulky that Saturday night, he had no interest in misty might-have-beens. Bessie had been implicated in a similar suspicious death and gotten off. He would not allow that to happen again.

I REACHED THE village of East Hampton and pulled into a spot opposite Lion Gardiner and his burial ground. Then I took out my phone. I suspected that Charles Tremaine would be at his office in Manhattan, and got the number from 411.

"Tremaine and Tyler Books," the receptionist chirped.

Tyler? "Is Charles there?"

"Who's calling, please?"

"One of his clients. Delhi Laine."

"I'll see if he's available." She switched me to Handel's Water Music.

"Hello, there." Charles sounded pleased to hear from me, but why wouldn't he be?

"I have some information for you. If you have some information for me."

"What's that?" A shade warier.

"There's been another attack at Adam's Revenge. The Farm, as you call it."

"What? No! Who?"

"The last time I saw you we talked about the au pair. Sonia. You told me you didn't know what happened to her. But I think you do."

Silence. "I only know what was in the local papers. It didn't even make *Newsday*."

"What did they say?"

"Evidently she had been drinking at the Farm and passed out. When she came to she realized she'd mistakenly drunk a container of lye."

"My God!"

"It destroyed her vocal cords."

"When did this happen? Is she still around?"

"It was about a month before Nate died. I have no idea where she is now. Period." He sounded as implacable as someone slamming the door on a Jehovah's Witness.

"Okay. There was a fire in Rosa Erikson's cottage in the early morning. It burned down, and she's in the hospital."

"No. Really? What's going on over there?"

I hesitated. "The fire was set deliberately."

"Get out! By whom?"

"The police are trying to find out."

"Rosa—she's the shy one, isn't she? Why would anybody want to do that?"

"A lot of strange stuff is going on."

I let him think about that, then asked, "Did you know that Nate Erikson's eyesight was failing?"

"I knew he had a problem. A chemical in Vietnam he was exposed to."

"Did he have someone helping him with his illustrations?"

"*Helping* him? Not that I ever heard. It's not like he needed a seeing-eye dog. Are they saying that Gretchen's death isn't an accident either?"

I gave him as many details as I could. "Who's Tyler?"

"My roommate from Yale."

We said good-bye.

CHAPTER FORTY-FOUR

THE OFFICES OF the *Hampton Beacon* were located in Southampton, a lively village I had always liked. I parked behind the Parrish Museum but did not go in, or wander through any of the nearby galleries. Instead, I went straight to the newspaper offices around the corner on Main Street.

"Unprepossessing" was the word. The room looked more like a neighborhood print shop than a working newspaper. A woman with cropped gray hair smiled at me from behind a high counter. "Hi there. Need to place an ad?"

"Actually I was looking for a back issue."

She thought that over. "Which one?"

"I'm not sure. Do you have an archive?"

"Oh, my dear, no. I guess we should, but—we have back issues, but not in any viewable order. You could try the library, but if you don't have a date . . . What are you looking for?"

I hesitated. "I'm doing some research on Nate Erikson. I'm trying to find out about someone who worked there. An au pair, Sonia?"

The smile disappeared so quickly that I was afraid she would order me out.

"That story? We didn't run it in *our* paper. Whatever happened was a tragedy and a disgrace. A young girl's life was ruined."

I thought about what to ask, how to ask it.

"If you can't speak, you can't teach or clerk, you can't even waitress! Think about that."

I did. "Where is she now?"

I expected to hear that Sonia had returned to her native land, wherever that was, or that she had disappeared from view.

"She has a little cottage in Amagansett that used to be a cabana. Someone—I don't know who—bought it for her afterward. She supports herself, if you can call it that, by washing dishes at the Shake Shack and making quilts."

Quilts. Who was I talking to recently about quilts?

Lynn, of course. Claude had blamed her for bringing Sonia to the compound.

"Does she live right on the beach?"

"No, the cabana was moved across Bluff Road years ago. It had originally been renovated as a guesthouse."

I thanked her and left without asking more questions. How many remodeled cabanas could there be?

I FOUND THE little house with no trouble. I had been imagining a shed, but this was guesthouse size, charmingly refinished with white clapboard and little window boxes filled with red impatiens. Instead of going in, I sat in my van, staring at it for several minutes. Did I have the right to knock on her door and rock this young woman's world again?

Belatedly I noticed a paved path leading to the house with a green VW Beetle parked on its hard-packed sand. On the driver's side was a colorful decal of a large daisy that made me sad. What kind of life could someone unable to speak have here, trying to eke out a living? I hoped she at least drew solace from being so near the ocean, from being able to walk along the shore every day. People even drew inspiration from beaches in winter, finding comfort in the snow-crested dunes, the stiff briny air, and the solitude.

I told myself I was romanticizing her situation and stepped out of the van. The saltwater smell on the September breeze carried me back to childhood summers at the Jersey shore, to the cottage we always rented in Ocean Grove. I remembered the sweetness of coconut-oil lotion, the taste of molasses-flavored taffy, the early-morning bike rides on the boardwalk before anyone else was up. The broken white clamshells on the path to Sonia's cottage were identical to the ones I remembered. A seagull, unimpressed by how near to him I was passing, poked at something in the reedy sand.

Once I was at Sonia's pale green door, I saw that the impatiens in the window boxes had gotten leggy and stretched. Soon they would have to be pulled out.

When Sonia came to the door, I was relieved to see she didn't look that much like me. We were the same height and had the same coloring, her hair was blond and tangled in waves like mine, but that was all. Her small, upturned nose and curved mouth contained an infectious joy that made you want to smile back. I could see her as Nellie Forbush in *South Pacific* or Laurey in *Oklahoma!*

I did smile back. "Hi. I'm Delhi Laine. I'm sorry to bother you, but I wanted to ask you something."

She inclined her head.

"Can I come in?"

Doubtful.

"I'm working over at the Erikson compound and bad things have been happening. Gretchen was killed and Rosa's cottage was set on fire."

The large gray-blue eyes, dark-flecked and intelligent, widened, and she pulled back the door for me to step inside.

Sonia lived in one large room. The furniture in the front area was brown wicker with flowered cushions. But we didn't sit. Instead we stood near the entrance next to a white iMac with a keyboard below. She leaned over and typed on it, then stood back so I could read it.

Tell me what happened.

I did. When I talked about Gretchen's death she looked sad. The details of Rosa's burnt cottage disturbed her more.

What did poor Rosa ever do to anyone? she typed. *Is there anything left?*

"I don't know if everything inside the cottage was destroyed." I hoped not. "Are you still in touch with the family?"

Maybe not a tactful question, but she wrote, *Lynn does everything for me. Lynn helped me get this place and found me my car. She knew I would need a car living out here.*

"Do you help her with her quilts?"

I piece them together for her and she does the quilting. The income really helps.

She gestured at the back corner of the cottage, opposite a cooking alcove. I looked and saw a sewing machine and stacks of fabric.

"That's great."

It keeps me busy. And my therapist wants me to write down everything that happened as I remember it. She said it will make me feel better to get it all out.

"Speaking of that, I wanted to ask you about what happened to you. If you don't mind."

She didn't turn back to the keyboard for a while, just stared deeper into the cottage.

"It's okay. You don't have to tell me."

She was back at the machine again, typing quickly now.

I want to help, but I still don't know what happened. I was in bed, asleep, and I woke up with my throat on fire and saw someone leaving my room. They made up a story that I had been drinking and drank a caustic by mistake. But I wasn't drunk, I'd only had some wine.

And there she stopped and turned back to me.

"Did you see who it was leaving?"

She added a name and gave me a somber look.

I felt sick. "I'm so sorry."

CHAPTER FORTY-FIVE

BECAUSE THE DAY was overcast, I willed it to get dark early. I needed the cover of night for the other thing I wanted to do. I wasn't going to drive all the way home and back out again, so I spent the time checking the local thrift shops and library sale shelves for books. Nothing exceptional, but I collected enough good titles to fill a cardboard carton.

At 6 p.m. I retreated to the Golden Pear Cafe and settled in with butternut squash soup and a tomato-mozzarella sandwich on a baguette. I could finally read *Let the Great World Spin* uninterrupted, and I lingered as people moved in and out, carrying away dinner. At 7:25, when the dusk seemed permanent, I headed back to Adam's Revenge. Tonight I drove past the compound and parked farther down the road, next to a barrier of oak trees. I opened the glove compartment and took out the small flashlight I kept for illuminating books in unlit basements.

There was no mistaking my white van with its "Got Books?" logo, but there was no reason for anyone from the family to drive down the road beyond the house. I locked the van and began to edge through the trees without turning my flashlight on, nearly tripping on one high root. From below the houses I could see that the lights were on in Claude and Lynn's cottage and in Bianca's chalet, as well as in the main house. I thought about Eve in there without Bessie or Gretchen for company, and wondered if Puck was home. What a change for her from the days when Nate was alive, the house filled with artists and conversation and laughter. What I had been seeing was the cast after the play was over, the theater empty, no one quite sure what to do next.

I had left the cover of trees and was approaching the shell of Rosa's cottage as quietly as I could when I heard a sound as stealthy as I was trying to be.

Nowhere to hide. I dropped to the ground and stretched out flat. The weeds were high here, the field unmowed, though anyone looking carefully would have seen the bump my body made. I couldn't see the cottage without raising my head and I didn't want to do that.

There was the crunch of someone trying to walk quietly across the ashes.

The hell with it. I lifted my head enough to see a woman's back beyond the yellow warning tape, moving away from me. The beam of her flashlight illuminated the ground and bounced up enough for me to see that she was wearing a hooded sweatshirt. I assumed it was a woman, but it could have been Puck's slender body as well. The only one it couldn't be was Bessie.

Then the light was extinguished and I heard nothing else. Had she found what she was looking for? If so, the item was small enough to carry in a pocket. I wondered if it was the same thing I wanted to see. What I didn't know was whether she'd be back. I had to move quickly.

When I got to where the back door had been, the acrid odor was unbearable. I hesitated, looking in. What had been a narrow pathway through the kitchen and into the hall was now obliterated by fallen objects. For a moment I wondered why everything looked wet, then remembered that the fire department had hosed everything down.

I stepped over the threshold where the harvest table had been, and caught my breath. Shards of white china shone everywhere like broken pieces of moon. Could any of Rosa's work be salvaged? I thought fleetingly about trying to rescue her plates. But it was impossible to breathe without choking, and I knew I couldn't stay.

The police had created a makeshift pathway farther into the kitchen and I picked my way along it, stumbling once or twice because I didn't want to use the flashlight. When I pressed the switch briefly, I saw that the whatnot with its china animals was barely damaged, suggesting that the fire had been set around the perimeter and had not gotten too far in.

When I reached the living room, I moved toward the corner where I had seen Gretchen's paintings, stacked against the wall.

The wall was no longer there.

The rubble could have held the painting I was looking for, but it was impossible to be sure. Then I remembered that the model had been Rosa's dead mother and hated the thought of her finding that out too.

If she survived.

DRIVING HOME, MY sweatshirt streaked with soot where I had brushed against furniture in the dark, I consoled myself with "at leasts." At least I had gotten out of the cottage without being discovered. What would the hooded figure have done if she had found me inside? At least I had seen the painting in Rosa's cottage last week. I couldn't prove anything now, but if I could make one or two more things fit the picture that was forming, Marselli would have to see it too.

CHAPTER FORTY-SIX

I WASN'T INVITED to lunch the next day.

I wouldn't have gone anyway.

Bianca came to the studio around three. "How's it
going?" She was dressed in the same peach sweater and
jeans as the first day I saw her, her ginger hair in a single
braid on her neck.

"Good. I'm just finishing up."

"Really? You won't forget about doing the photos, will
you?"

I was surprised. "You still want me to?"

"Why wouldn't I? I was thinking that maybe you
could use one or two pictures of Morgan. She was so cute,
and—the book is for her, after all."

"That's a great idea."

"I have some black-and-white photos that a friend of
my father's took. I'm sure you could do something about
tinting them."

"Not a problem."

She hovered beside the door. "We found out that Bessie wasn't in jail when Rosa's cottage burned down. They had been questioning her and let her go. I think Rosa saw something, maybe Bessie putting Gretchen in the pool, and Bessie was afraid Rosa would turn her in."

It was an interesting theory. "I think I know what happened."

"What?"

"I'm still working the details out."

When she saw that I wasn't going to tell her anything else, she left.

I SOLDIERED ON, hoping to be done before seven, but all too soon it was dark outside. I still had to make sure that I had examined all the books, and leave everything exactly as I had found it. While I checked the shelves, I wondered if I should call Marselli and tell him what I thought. He would not be receptive. He would demand proof. When he had things worked out, he did not like to be contradicted. I decided to call him anyway.

I was reaching for my bag to find my phone when I was overpowered by another feeling. *Get out of here. Leave. Now.* I could work out the final logistics of the evaluation and how to present it to the Eriksons back in the barn. Staying around after telling Bianca that I thought I knew what happened was crazy, it was putting myself in danger. I had wanted to see how she would react, but what was I thinking? This was not an English drawing room where everyone gathered politely to listen to the denouement.

I honestly believed I could pack up my laptop, store the flash drives in my bag, climb into my van, and drive home. I was opening the door with one hand, reaching for the light switch with the other, when a voice from the darkness said, "I was wondering when you'd come out."

Eve's white hair floated around her pale, creased face, hair light as dandelion fluff, and her ice blue eyes were steady on mine. There was no fog in them now. I stared down at the hand holding a kitchen knife close to my stomach. She gestured at me to go back inside and I did.

She followed me, slamming the door behind her hard. "I know you think you're clever. But I've known you were in here since the beginning. Do you really think I don't know everything that goes on around here?"

Did I think that? I guessed I had. "Bianca said I could use the studio to work on our project."

"My *husband's* studio? And did she say you could rearrange all the books and put them in cartons? What are my treacherous children up to now?" A flash of silver near the hip of her navy slacks. Her arm had relaxed but the point of the knife was still nearby. "Tell me, or you won't leave here alive."

It was so melodramatic I almost laughed. I knew I could overpower her before she could inflict any real damage. "They wanted me to look at the books, that's all. Libraries should be cataloged."

"And they're *paying* you for this. With my money."

"Is it?"

She gave a snort, a little laugh. Why had I let the family deceive me into believing she was incompetent? Perhaps because it was a role she enjoyed playing.

"Nate's children, still sucking at the tit. They can't be using their money, they don't have any."

I was confused. "But they're your children too. I thought you wanted to keep them living close by."

"You thought so, did you? You don't know anything."

"I know you slashed the painting of Sonia."

Guilty.

"And that you poured lye down Sonia's throat to get her away from Nate."

"Sonia—that little nobody? He was finished with her, he told me so himself. Nate never kept anything from me. He had been tempted, she was a handful all right, but he knew he was too old to start over. Some pair they would have made—he couldn't see and she couldn't talk." Her mouth twisted.

"Maybe he changed his mind." I looked over at the white cup and saucer still on the studio table. "Did you put something in his coffee to make him pass out when he was swimming?" I had already worked out why she had not saved Morgan. Without the child there could be no more young and pretty au pairs. Maybe Morgan had been the target and Nate had tried unsuccessfully to intervene. It was not as if Eve was physically related to the little girl.

"Did you burn the picture of Morgan and Nate?"

"Terrible shot." She gave an impatient wave with her knife hand as if she had destroyed it because it offended her artistic sensibilities.

"Gretchen was going to expose you at the memorial," I said. "Or maybe claim credit for the work *she* had done on the illustrations. And that would have destroyed the whole mystique." Gretchen's painting that had seemed so familiar to me in Rosa's cottage, the woman in the white blouse, *was* familiar. It was the same face as Queen Esther in my Bible storybook.

Eve pursed her mouth. "Do you really think anyone cares about that now?"

The door creaked behind her. "Delhi, are you still here?"

Eve whirled around, inches from Bianca. "You're just as bad!"

"Mama, what are you doing here?"

But Eve had had enough. Still holding the knife, she pushed against Bianca on her way out the door. Bianca screamed as the blade slid into her side. And then Eve was gone.

CHAPTER FORTY-SEVEN

BIANCA, ARMS FLAILING, was trying to pull the knife out. I was trying to stop her, grabbing for her hands, keeping them away from the hilt. The knife had sunk deep.

"But. It. Hurts."

"Lie down. Just lie down here."

"No, it hurts," she moaned, and grabbed for the knife again.

By holding on to her narrow shoulders and moving her deeper into the studio, I was able to press her down onto the studio floor. Her peach sweater was darkening on her lower left side, a red pool spreading fast. *What to do, what to do.*

I pulled off my gray "Port Lewis" sweatshirt and wrapped the cloth around the knife, then pressed down hard on either side of the hilt.

Bianca yelped at the pressure.

Was I doing the right thing? Maybe the pressure

would make the blood spurt out faster. People wrapped injuries with tourniquets, but I had nothing to go around her entire stomach.

"Here, hold your hands like this, while I get my phone." I brought her hands over to the wound, but there was no pressure in them.

My fingers were shaking, but I managed to pull my bag off the table and get my phone out. Then, still kneeling next to Bianca, I dialed 911.

"Nine-one-one."

"Please, someone's been stabbed. We need help right away!"

"Your name?"

"That doesn't matter, just *send* someone!"

"Stay calm. Where are you located?"

"In Springs. On Cooper's Farm Lane."

"Number?"

"I don't *know*. It's a big house, the Erikson house." I panicked because I didn't know how to tell her how to find the studio. "Someone will be out on the road waiting for you."

Bianca's breathing had gotten harsh.

"Please hurry," I begged.

"Is he conscious?"

"She. Yes."

"Is there much bleeding?"

"Yes—we need help!"

"Don't move the victim. Someone will be there as soon as possible. I'll keep checking back with you." She clicked off.

Bianca's hands had slid limply off her sweater and the stain of blood was spreading. Frantically I pressed down firmly with both palms above and below the knife hilt.

She gave another gasp and her eyes moved to the side.

"Someone is coming. Just hang on."

But I couldn't leave her. She didn't have the strength to provide any compression. Worse, if I wasn't there she might pull out the knife completely to stop the pain, causing gushes of blood and certain death.

How could this be happening? Impossible that Bianca would die.

Moving my right hand away from the wound, I groped for my phone. "Bianca? What's Claude's number?"

She closed her eyes and moaned.

"Bianca? Tell me the number! We have to call him."

Miraculously, she did, though she stumbled over the words.

I punched the numbers in, and pushed speakerphone. Then I went back to pressing Bianca's stomach. The red circle on her sweater seemed to be crusting, without as much new blood. But what did I know about blood flow and first aid?

"Hello?"

"Lynn? Lynn, Bianca's been *hurt*. In the studio. The ambulance is coming, but someone needs to be by the road to show them where to come. Now."

"What happened?"

"Just *go*. If they can't find her right away, she'll—" I didn't finish. I waited for the click as Lynn hung up.

Immediately the phone rang again. I pressed the green symbol with a bloody thumb.

"How are you doing?" the 911 operator asked into the room.

"We're okay." *I hope.*

"She still conscious?"

"I think so."

"Keep her talking. They're on the way."

The click of disconnect.

For a moment I couldn't think of anything to talk about. Bianca's face was already white, her freckles like blood pricks.

"It's going to be fine. You're going to be fine."

"Why did she . . ."

"It was an accident. You were in her way."

"Am I going to die?" she whispered.

"Of course not! You have to relax—no, don't move."

Her eyes closed. She seemed to be having trouble breathing now.

"Bianca, let's think about the illustrations you want in your book."

"My book?" It was a whisper.

"You know. Your poems. Your wonderful poems."

Dear God, don't let her die. Don't let her die, don't let her die.

CHAPTER FORTY-EIGHT

WHEN THE DOOR creaked open and banged back against the wall, the floor dropped away beneath me. Eve was back with another knife. While I was trying to protect Bianca she would stab me and we would both die. I made myself look anyway and saw Claude and Lynn escorting a small army into the room.

Voices, a confusion of technicians carrying equipment, blue-suited police. Claude and Lynn stepped back against the wall, looking terrified. I pushed myself up from the floor, wanting to weep with relief when the technicians took over. I had probably done everything wrong, but they would know what to do. I fought the urge to retreat to a corner and sit with my hands over my face.

Everyone was demanding to know what happened.

"Are you hurt?" An East Hampton town policeman with grizzled graying hair was staring at my blood-spattered sweatshirt.

"No, I'm okay." I looked down at my hands still covered in Bianca's blood and pressed them on the table to keep standing upright.

"Tell me what happened."

"Her mother—stabbed her."

"Where's the mother now?"

"I don't know. She ran off."

"Mama?" Claude interrupted us, shocked. "Are you talking about my mother?" Incongruously he was wearing his maroon dressing gown over his slacks, and leather slippers.

The policeman ignored him. "She had a knife?"

"She came to see who was in her husband's studio."

"She thought someone had broken in?"

"I don't know what she thought." I swayed and leaned heavily on the table. "She started talking, starting rambling about her husband and the au pair and—"

"Don't listen to her," Claude cried, his thin face pained. "Since my father's death, my mother's had all kinds of fantasies about what happened. I doubt she was even in the studio tonight."

The policeman stared at him. "Well, somebody stabbed her." He gestured at Bianca and we all turned to watch two EMTs in light green scrubs lift the stretcher from the floor. A third seemed to be clearing a path though no one was in the way, and opened the door. As Bianca passed us I tried to tell how she was by the way she looked. But she was already hooked up to tubing and had an oxygen mask over her face.

As soon as Bianca was gone, Claude thrust a hand

toward me but spoke to the policeman. "She's lying about my mother. My mother couldn't have been here, she's an invalid. She's been asleep in the house for hours. This woman and my sister obviously had a fight, probably over money. She got angry and stabbed Bianca, then got worried and called for help."

Even though I knew Bianca could tell them what had actually happened, I felt a splash of terror. What if she never regained consciousness and I was arrested? There were no other witnesses to explain what had happened and I didn't expect Eve to confess. I knew in the confusion I had grabbed the knife hilt. What had Regan said about innocent people being railroaded for crimes they never committed? Bianca would die and I would go to jail. "I'm calling Frank Marselli!"

"You're not calling anyone," the policeman said gruffly.

"But he's the detective on another case here. He's with Homicide."

"Suffolk County?"

"Yes! Out of Hauppauge." I looked around for my small silver phone, then saw it on the worktable, still smeared with blood. I was too weak to reach over and pick it up. Instead I inched around the worktable and collapsed on the metal stool, propping up my head. Finally I picked the phone up and scrolled down. When Marselli's name appeared, I punched the dial button. My hand was shaking so much I could barely hold the receiver close enough to my mouth.

The phone rang into an evidently empty room, and

I thought of all the unimportant times I'd been able to reach him. Now when I needed him most, when everything was a matter of life and death . . . I waited for a prompt to let me speak to someone else. Finally another officer picked up and identified himself.

"My name is Delhi Laine," I mumbled. "Please tell Frank Marselli to come out to Springs to the Eriksons. Eve Erikson stabbed her daughter."

"It's not true," Claude cried. His pale face had taken on an odd reddish blush. He grabbed the policeman's arm. "This 'detective' you let her call, he's her *boyfriend*. He'll believe any story she tells him. She's threatened my sister before."

The policeman looked at me, betrayed.

I shook my head. I could not begin to explain anything. What if Claude actually believed what he was saying? Marselli was my only hope.

"Okay, let's calm down here. We'll sort things out when he gets here."

"Whatever you say. I'm going to check that my mother is okay."

"Sir, no one is leaving right now." He glanced over to the door where the younger policeman stood guard and gave a nod.

And so we waited.

It reminded me of the times I had taken my children to the emergency room with fractures or high temperatures or to get stitches. Lynn stood on Claude's far side, looking stricken, but keeping her thoughts to herself. Claude spent the time glowering at me, now and then giving his head a quick shake, as if my lies were not to be believed.

I wanted to annihilate him.

The nauseating smell of Bianca's blood lingered in the room.

Finally I heard the door open. But it was only Puck, who had seen the police car and lights on in the studio. I saw the younger cop bar his way, then step outside to talk to him.

"Ask him to check on my mother," Claude called after them. "Make sure she's okay."

Back to silence. I wondered where Eve was now. Would she admit to stabbing Bianca? A further, frightening thought: Would she even remember?

In a moment the younger cop came back in alone. He had nothing to report.

MARSELLI ARRIVED A few minutes after nine. He looked as if he had come from home, in jeans, a Special Olympics T-shirt, tan windbreaker, and black Nikes.

He took in the scene, then moved to the older policeman, flipping open his ID. "Who's the stabbing vic?"

"Young woman, name of Bianca Erikson."

"Witnesses?"

He jerked his head at me.

"Figures," Marselli muttered.

That did not bolster my confidence.

"She's the one who did it!" Claude broke in.

I still couldn't tell if he believed that. He was making up the story that Bianca and I ever fought about money. Yet what had she told him when I asked to be paid? Had she said that I was *demanding* money? Why had I ever brought it up? Surely he was just upset that I had accused his mother. If someone had accused my mother of a crime, I would be disbelieving and look around for someone else to blame.

Marselli jerked his head at the older policeman and they went into a private huddle over by the fireplace. Marselli seemed to be doing most of the talking. When he returned to us, he said to Claude, "Did you see what happened?"

"Of course not! She was the one who called and told us what she had done."

I opened my mouth, but Marselli waved me quiet.

Lynn spoke up. "She said we should wait for the ambulance and bring them down to the studio, which we did. All she said was that Bianca was hurt."

"Okay, you can go. Good-bye."

But now Claude seemed cemented to the floor. Lynn pulled at his arm and pried him loose. At the door, he turned. "Don't believe anything she says about my mother. She's lying to save her own skin."

"Not a fan of yours," Marselli said when he was gone.

"No." I felt too weak to explain anything, but I made myself tell Marselli what had happened when Eve came to the studio. It was hard to admit, but I added, "I guess I upset her more. I accused her of murdering her husband because he was having an affair with the babysitter and then killing Gretchen so that she wouldn't tell anyone. But I think that's what really happened." I stopped talking and my eyes pooled. "If Bianca doesn't make it . . ."

He studied my face. "She's critical?"

"She lost so much blood. Those other policemen wouldn't let me call the hospital to find out."

That wasn't totally true. But they had told me I couldn't call anyone.

"She's at Southampton?"

"That's what somebody said."

He called his office and asked to be put through to the hospital. I could hear only his side of the conversation. "E-R-I-K-S-O-N, Bianca."

A pause, a couple of "Uh-huhs," more listening, and then, "Okay, thanks."

I knew he was going to tell me she had died. Instead he gave me a slight smile. "She's out of surgery. She'll be okay. Fortunately someone here kept her from bleeding out."

I assumed he was talking about her rescue by the EMTs, then realized he meant me.

All the fears I had been holding in spilled over. I put my face in my hands and sobbed.

"B-I-A-N-C-A, Blanca."

CHAPTER FORTY-NINE

"YOU HAVE TO tell me," Bianca insisted. "Tell me exactly
what she said."

I shifted in the green vinyl visitor's chair. Even though
Bianca was out of danger, they were keeping her in the
hospital to monitor her for infection. She was still paler
than normal, and her ice blue eyes were tugged at by lines
I had never noticed before.

Earlier that morning I had given Marselli a detailed
statement of what Eve had said in the studio. But as he
had pointed out to me, Eve had said very little that was
incriminating. I had been the one making accusations
and she had never denied them. They were holding her for
stabbing Bianca. Because the autopsy found that Gretchen
had been drugged, they were checking Eve's pharma-
ceuticals to see if any matched what had been found in
Gretchen's system.

"She was upset about your father and Sonia," I told Bianca now.

"Really? I thought that was over. It was just a flirtation on his part. I guess she took it more seriously. My father could have that effect on people. Sometimes he seemed larger than life."

There was the scrape of feet on linoleum outside the door, and I turned to see Claude and Lynn staring at me. Claude grasped his wife's arm as if marshaling the strength to rescue his sister.

"What are you doing here?" he demanded. "I want you out of here now!"

"Wait outside please, Claude," Bianca said. "We're talking."

"But you don't know what she's done."

"You mean saved my life? After Mama stabbed me?"

"It wasn't Mama. She—"

"Claude, I *know* what happened. I was there, okay?" Her cheeks had developed two bright red circles that were not a healthy color. "Wait outside. You too, Lynn."

Claude scowled, but they disappeared from sight.

"He keeps insisting it was me," I complained. It sounded childish as soon as I said it.

"Of course it wasn't you. It was my mother. But it was an accident. She must have seen the lights on in the studio and thought an intruder had gotten in. She had the knife to protect herself. It was the first time you had stayed until dark. Unfortunately she was holding the knife when she ran into me. Why don't the police believe that? Puck said they arrested her!"

"They didn't arrest her. They're questioning her. After all, you almost . . . didn't make it." I was sure Eve hadn't meant to hurt Bianca so badly. But I had seen her flash of pique, her anger at Bianca's role in my being there, as she pressed the knife toward her.

"How can they blame someone for an accident?"

I looked at her and knew she wasn't strong enough to hear the truth. She looked so thin and insubstantial in her hospital gown. "They need to ask her questions about Gretchen."

"Bessie . . ."

"Bessie may have helped by carrying the body downstairs and out to the pool. But your mother . . ."

Bianca reared back. "That's impossible. Did Bessie blame my mother? I thought she loved Mama."

Not enough to go to jail for her. The problem was, as soon as Bessie had been released from questioning, she and her whole family had headed south. Their neighbors told police that they had relatives in Mississippi, but no one knew any names or places—at least none that they were willing to share.

"My mother would *never* hurt Gretchen."

"Bianca, I never said that. But she did pour lye down Sonia's throat."

"What are you talking about?" Now she looked puzzled. "Sonia drank it herself. My mother wasn't even here when it happened. She was down in Charleston. My grandfather had had a heart attack and she flew down. She was there for a week."

"Are you sure?"

"Of course I'm sure, I was here when it happened last May. It was a terrible accident, but my mother didn't have anything to do with it."

Had I gotten everything wrong?

CHAPTER FIFTY

WHEN I CAME into the hall, Claude and Lynn were leaning against the pale yellow wall. Both of them looked
tired. He pushed up from the wall like a coiled spring.

Quickly I said, "Claude, Bianca needs to tell you
something."

He gave Lynn an I-told-you-so look and bumped past me.

As soon as he was gone, I said to Lynn, "I have to talk
to you. It's important."

She didn't look surprised. "I'm already late for the
shelter, but—you could come there in about an hour. It's
called A Safe Haven. In Sag Harbor."

"Okay, fine."

"Let me give you directions. We try to keep the location a secret. Woman in trouble have a phone number
they can call." She told me how to find the shelter, then
added, "Come around eleven-thirty. Before noon anyway.
I'll be in my office."

A SAFE HAVEN was located on a residential street of large homes in Sag Harbor. With its widow's walk, the cupola where an anxious wife could stand and scan the harbor for signs of her husband's ship, there was little to distinguish this house from the other sea captains' homes. Most had historic plaques by the front doors.

I went up wide wooden steps flanked by fading pink hydrangeas, and knocked on the paneled door.

Lynn herself answered and brought me down a hall. We passed a large room, its pocket doors slightly ajar. I was startled to hear feral grunts and cries from inside.

Lynn laughed. "It's a self-defense class." She kept going until we came to a small parlor near the end. The bay window on the side facing the house next door gave the room a formal feeling, but the stiff Victorian furniture had been changed out for soft hand-me-downs. Several framed prints from *Godey's Lady's Book* made the room feel reassuring. I sank into the sofa and Lynn took a chair on my right.

"We had an incident last year that made us supercareful. We keep our location secret, but an ex-husband followed his wife, his former wife, home from a prenatal visit and shot her on the steps outside."

"My God! Did she . . ."

"Yes, and she left behind a two-year-old. We still don't know how he knew about her doctor's appointment. It really made us ratchet up security though." She looked pensive, then added, "You said you had something important."

"It's about Sonia."

Her mouth curved into a reluctant smile. "It's not like I'm a priest or therapist, but—I'll tell you as much as I can."

"Thank you."

"Sonia came here after she was beaten up by the man she lived with. Not the first time. He was older than she was, an important figure on Broadway, and she had come here from Minnesota to act. So she put up for him too long. The old story, he was obsessive and then abusive. Meanwhile, she had no money. She needed a job and a place to stay, and Bianca needed someone to help with Morgan. I thought it would be a perfect match. Except that . . ."

"She got involved with Nate."

"So you know about that. I still don't know how serious he was. He was flattered and she was completely smitten. And she was accessible, living right on the compound. When Eve had to go down to Charleston for a week, Sonia was in the studio every night. Everyone knew it."

"Even Rosa."

Lynn laughed and pulled at a thread on the arm of the chair she was sitting in. "Even Rosa. I tried to talk to Sonia about being more discreet, but she was over the top. She was so sure they would be together forever. She assumed he would tell Eve to go back to South Carolina, but I knew that would never happen."

"The lye?"

"Nate had a thing about animals, all kinds. I think I told you that. He was certain that Rosa's stuff was attracting vermin, so he had a rat poison, lye-based, that he secretly mixed and poured outside her cottage. That night he had a coffee can of it on his table to use later."

I started at that, afraid of where the story was headed. Sonia had told me Eve had poured the lye down her throat, but she had been in Charleston and couldn't have. If Lynn told me *Nate* had actually been the one who made Sonia drink it, I could never look at another of his illustrations.

"It was the night before Eve was coming back, and Nate told Sonia that as wonderful as it had been, things had to end. He hinted that she might have to leave Adam's Revenge. Of course Sonia was frantic at that, she grabbed the can from his table thinking it was turpentine and said if he didn't love her she didn't want to live. It was just a gesture, she only drank a little, but it wasn't turpentine, it was pure caustic. She passed out from the pain and woke up in the hospital with her life ruined."

"She didn't want to go home, wherever that was?"

"Minnesota. No. I helped her all I could. She needed a place to stay and a way to get around, so we worked that out. Nate bought the cottage for her outright. He was devastated. And she helps with my quilts."

"She told me Eve poured the lye down her throat."

Lynn sighed. "She hated Eve. And she was probably embarrassed to admit that she had done it herself. And I've probably talked way too much."

"I think it's great that you're helping her."

She gave me her warm smile. "Someone did it once for me. I was engaged to a guy I met in college, but he turned vicious and I couldn't break away from him. I was heavier than I am now, I think I felt that no one else would ever want me. But after he nearly choked me to death I got rid of him and a year later met Claude. I know, Claude seems a little . . . eccentric to you, but he would *never* do anything to hurt me. Ever. He loves me. When I see how gentle he is with the dog, it reminds me why I married him."

"He's a good man."

We sat there thinking good thoughts about Claude.

Then I left to confront Sonia.

CHAPTER FIFTY-ONE

BECAUSE I WASN'T sure what to do next, I called Marty on his cell phone.

"Campagna!"

"Hi Marty, it's Delhi."

"Delhi who?"

"Ha. I've finished the appraisal and you'll *love* these books. And you can afford them. They'll probably go for auction at Phillips. Anyway, you should at least talk to Susie."

"Why?"

"Because you want to open your shop. Because she's good and I can't do it. I said I'd help get things started, but we need to sit down and figure out how this is going to work. It's going to be great."

"Explain to me again why I'm bringing her in."

"Because you are. How about tomorrow at two at the bookshop?"

"I'm not making any promises."

"Good. I'll see you then."

As I suspected, Susie's schedule was flexible enough for her to meet with us anytime.

I COULDN'T PUT off talking to Sonia any longer.

On the drive over to Amagansett, I wondered if she would be home. What time did her shift at the Shake Shack start? What a comedown, washing dishes instead of following her dream of acting. She hadn't seemed bitter . . . but I wondered.

When I reached Bluff Road, I saw only a few cars parked in front of the beach houses I passed. The VW with the daisy was in front of the cabana as well. I didn't want to pull in behind it, so I squeezed the van as far onto the sand as I could without getting stuck. I wasn't sure what the regulations about street parking were, but perhaps it didn't matter as much in late September. I didn't expect to be long.

I wasn't even sure what I was going to ask her. Start with why she had lied about Eve and take it from there.

When I reached the little house, I rapped on the front door, but no one answered. I listened and could hear no one moving around inside, then knocked again. Finally I reached out and tried the knob. The door opened halfway.

The light inside the room was a watery gray, the stacks of quilting material against the walls like a shadowy congregation. "Sonia?"

I stepped inside. The white laptop stood open on my right. I glanced at the icons, curious, but didn't move toward the machine. I hadn't come there to snoop.

Actually I had. I just didn't expect to get the chance.

Next to the computer was a list. I glanced down at it.

Toothpaste
Herbal Essence conditioner
Paper towels
Blue thread
Dan's Papers
Milk

Something about the handwriting was familiar, something about the way the O's slanted and looped at the top. Where had I seen O's like that recently? And then I remembered.

My hand hovered over the paper. I wanted to snatch it up, slide it in my bag, take it to Marselli. But I knew that would make it worthless as evidence of anything.

Instead I turned to the laptop screen.

There were few icons on the desktop. One of them was labeled "What Happened."

A metallic noise rang into the room and I jumped. It was only the older-style refrigerator in the kitchen alcove. Sighing, I waited for my heart to resume its usual worka-day rhythm, then moved back to the door and looked out. Sonia was nowhere in sight. Either she had gone for a walk on the beach or someone had given her a ride into town.

The only flash drive I had with me was the one with

the information about Nate Erikson's books. Even as I reached for it, I had a terrible fear that inserting it in Sonia's PC might ruin it, erase the content somehow. It would likely happen at the same time as someone was breaking into my van and stealing my laptop, the only other place I had the information.

But what was more important—losing two weeks' work or knowing the truth?

Holding my breath, I pressed my flash drive into the USB port and waited. In a moment the icon labeled "Erikson" flashed on the screen. I reached out and dragged the "What Happened" folder onto it—just as I heard a scraping on the stoop outside. *Come on, Come on.* I begged it.

There was squeak of the door being pulled open. Without even knowing if the file had finished copying, I yanked the flash drive out of her machine and dropped it in my bag. Then I turned to face an appalled Sonia.

"It's okay," I said quickly. "I came to tell you something important. I got cold waiting outside."

She was wearing a black hoodie with St. Olaf's College and a prancing lion on the front.

Think, Delhi. "Eve Erikson has been arrested for Gretchen's death. And Nate's."

She looked at me, taking in the words. And then she gave me a smile, the vindicated smile of Laurey when she realizes Curly loves her after all.

She turned to her computer to write a response, then stopped and frowned at me.

I moved over to see.

The message I had come to hate, the image of a red

octagonal with a white exclamation point in the center, was still on the screen: "The disk was not ejected properly. If possible always select Eject before unplugging or turning it off."

Damn. There had been no time to eject my flash drive properly. "Don't worry about that," I said. "It's nothing. I get that message all the time."

But Sonia was too smart for my lie. *What did you copy?* she typed.

"I didn't touch your computer. I—"

Before I could imagine it happening, she had whirled and grabbed my arms just above the elbows. She shoved me back against the entryway wall and held me pinned there.

"What did you copy?" It wasn't a voice, it was an unearthly mouse squeak, harsh and breathy at the same time, a terrible sound that I could never have deciphered if I had not guessed what she was saying. It was the sound I imagined someone being strangled to death would make in protest.

Sonia's hold on my arms was effective. I remembered the self-defense class I had passed at A Safe Haven, and wondered if she had learned it there. I fought hard to get loose, but she was younger than I and very strong. Unexpectedly she pulled me toward her, then banged my head against the wall.

For a moment the room blurred.

Another rush of strangled sounds. *Give it to me?*

What else would she be asking? I tried kicking out at her, but she stepped back and my foot grazed her leg.

With our faces so close, hers was terrifying. Something primal had taken over. Gone was the pretty, hopeful ingénue who evoked everyone's sympathy. Her blue eyes glittered and her mouth was slightly open almost in a smile, as if she were enjoying our struggle. Enjoying putting her expertise to use. There was an element of teasing, like an older sibling torturing a younger one. Yet I knew she wouldn't suddenly laugh, let me go, and say, *Don't tell Mom, okay?*

She knew what I had taken. She had to get her confession back, even if one of us died. And she knew it would not be her.

The back of my head was already aching. If she pulled me forward to bang my head again, I was ready for her.

But she didn't. She unclamped my arms and immediately brought her hands up to my throat. She pressed her thumbs into the center and I gagged. Desperately I tried to reach her face to scratch her and kneed her in the groin hard. In the momentary distraction that loosened her hands, I shoved my body against hers. We fell to the floor, Sonia banging her head on the opposite wall on the way down.

I had a millisecond to get away. Jamming my hand over her eyes and nose, I pushed myself up. The pressure had to be excruciating and she shrieked, a terrible sound. I was half standing when she grabbed at my leg and I nearly went back down. But I managed to kick at her and pull away, get the door open, and take two steps before I bumped into a solid form.

"Delhi, what are you doing?"

Lynn.

Sonia must have been right behind me, because Lynn said, "Sonia, are you okay? What's going on? Write it for me."

Lynn didn't realize that she had just saved my life. Sonia could not go on attacking me in front of her mentor. But she cried, "Stop her! She stole something from me."

As Lynn blinked, confused, and I moved around her and whispered, "Meet me in Starbucks in East Hampton."

Then I took my sore body and aching throat and half-limped, half-ran to my van.

But Sonia's unearthly howls pursued me. When I turned, I saw that Lynn was trying to hold Sonia back, pressing her against the door frame, Sonia had nearly broken free.

In the next moment she had. Perhaps I imagined the hiss and thud of someone running on the sand but I could feel her behind me.

Why had I parked so far away?

If she caught me, and I knew she could, Lynn could not save me again.

Chapter Fifty-Two

I WAS NEARLY to the van when I remembered I had locked the doors because my computer was inside. *No.*

If my keys were in my woven bag, I might as well stop right there and let her push my face into the sand. Yet I had known I might need to leave fast. Praying I had jammed them in my jacket pocket, I reached inside and pulled out a fistful of metal. *Thank you.*

I pressed the remote unlock button.

Now I was on the tarmac, wrenching open the driver's door and halfway inside when Sonia was there too, yanking on my arm, trying to topple me out. I squeezed the steering wheel in a death grip, then pressed my chest against the horn. The sudden blare was enough to startle her, giving me the chance to swing my left foot around and jam it hard against her chest.

Sonia staggered backward several feet, catching herself before she fell, but giving me the chance to close my door. Frantically I pressed the "lock" button.

She was back the next moment, yanking at the door handle. Her face through the glass was hideous now, red and contorted. When she found she could not get in, she pounded with her fists on the window.

Was she strong enough to break it?

Then she stepped back, looking behind her as if for a rock or piece of metal strong enough to shatter glass.

I didn't wait for her to find it. I turned the key and started the van as she tried to grab the door handle. Her fingers may have grazed it but they couldn't hold on.

ALTHOUGH I HAD no idea whether Lynn would meet me or how Sonia might explain everything to her, I drove to Starbucks in Easthampton. I had chosen the coffee shop because she would know it and because there were always a crowd of people inside. *Safety in numbers.*

Because it was early afternoon, past lunchtime, I was able to find a small wooden table with no trouble. I bought a cappuccino and settled myself against a wall facing into the room. Not that I needed caffeine. My adrenaline was still in the stratosphere, my heart just now realizing that it could calm down.

If death had been imminent, would I have given her the flash drive? Would it have mattered to her then? If what I suspected was true, then one more death would have made no difference to her.

I looked around the room. It was time to find out. I couldn't wait for Lynn to read "What Happened." Unzipping the black canvas bag, I brought out my laptop and opened it. My fingers were still shaking as I pressed the flash drive into the machine.

The first thing I found was that the Erikson file was unharmed. Then I opened Sonia's file and began reading. I scanned through how she had come to New York and met the abusive theater director. How she had gone to A Safe Haven and ended up at Adam's Revenge. She was in the middle of describing her life there when the door opened and I saw Lynn step over the threshold and look around. She came over to me quickly.

"You'd better tell me what's going on." She looked almost as angry as she had been when Puck had been cruel to Bianca about Morgan. "Sonia said you broke into her cottage!"

"I was waiting for her inside," I admitted.

"And then you *attacked* her. I have to tell you, she's going to press charges."

"I attacked her? You were there. You saw her run after me. You tried to stop her."

"She was just trying to get back what you took."

"I'll show you what it was. Can I get you something?" I looked toward the counter.

"Of course not! I had stopped by Sonia's to pick up a quilt she's working on for me, and I never expected anything like that." She loomed over me, a stern presence. "I should never have told you anything about her."

"Please sit down. I need to show you something."

Grudgingly she started to pull out a chair, then changed her mind. "I want a water. I'll get it myself."

I kept reading. I had just finished the section where

Sonia mistakenly drank the lye, when Lynn returned. She sat down and I turned my laptop so we both could read what followed:

> I kept waiting for Nate to come see me at the hospital and apologize—he should *never* have kept lye on his desk—but he never did. Finally I couldn't wait any longer and went to the compound to see *him*. I had to make him realize that now more than ever we needed to be together. I wrote out how I felt on a piece of paper and went early when I knew he would be swimming laps.
>
> He looked happy to see me. He came to the side of the pool and read my paper, and then said no. He couldn't leave Eve. He had his family and his reputation to think about. He was too old. I leaned over to kiss him anyway and when he got close I realized how unfair he was being and banged his head on the side. With both hands.
>
> I guess it knocked him out because he slipped under the water. I was going to go for help when Morgan came running to me out of nowhere. She was so happy to see me, but I had to push her away. She fell into the pool and I felt terrible, but I couldn't have her telling people she'd seen me there. I had to get away.
>
> I didn't remember the paper until I was safely home. But I hadn't signed my name, and nothing happened. Then Saturday Gretchen came to see me. She said she had seen a strange car parked on the road besides the woods that morning, but hadn't thought it was important

since the drownings were an accident. Then Thursday when she was dropping off some dry cleaning she saw me get out of that car and recognized it by the daisy on the door. That damned daisy! She wouldn't have remembered it otherwise, it had been three months.

Not only that, she said she had picked up a piece of paper by the pool when she found Nate and now that she knew I had driven there that morning she was sure it was my handwriting.

To calm her down I made her tea and put in the sedative they gave me at the hospital. When she started to get groggy I made her lie down on my bed. I think by then she knew what was happening to her. She told me she didn't have the paper anymore, but I got her to say she had given it to Rosa. The sedative was wearing off and she tried to get up, so I put my pillow over her face. I couldn't take her back until that night when everyone was at the memorial—yes, I still keep track of the family— and drove Gretchen's car back and put her in the pool to make it look like an accident.

It was too weird driving with a dead body in the car. I parked by the woods and dragged her over to the pool, but then I couldn't find the paper in her room. The trouble with such a tangled web is that there's never any end, even when it's not your fault. But I wasn't going to hurt anyone else. I made sure Rosa was outside when I burned the paper inside her cottage. No more deaths, though they had all been accidents.

I just have to find the strength to go on.

It ended there.

"Where did you get this?" Lynn whispered.

"From Sonia's laptop."

"This paper she keeps talking about?"

"The police have it. Rosa gave it to me to keep. I didn't know what it was until today when I saw a list Sonia had made and saw it was the same handwriting."

Lynn looked at me, as anguished as if she had caused a fatal crash. "It's all my fault! I was the one who brought her there and she *killed* everyone."

"Come on, Lynn. You didn't force Nate to get involved with her."

"It's still my fault."

"You can't predict how life will turn out."

I don't know if she heard me. Elbows on the table, she covered her face with her hands.

While Lynn wept quietly, I called Frank Marselli and insisted he come out to East Hampton. Now.

MARSELLI AND THE East Hampton police went to the cabana that same night. Sonia was in the process of loading up the Beetle to head home for Minnesota. They brought her in for questioning instead and confiscated her computer. She maintained, Marselli told me, that none of it had been her fault.

CHAPTER FIFTY-THREE

I NEARLY FORGOT the meeting at the bookstore the next afternoon. Hurriedly I picked up a bottle of Chardonnay and some plastic cups, then stopped at La Bonne Chance Boulangerie. I felt nearly as nervous as I had when I had introduced Colin to my parents all those years ago. They had been ready to dislike him for interrupting my education. They knew that we would be getting married and traveling to archeological sites, but they didn't yet know about Jane.

I was nearly at the bookshop door when Susie emerged from where she had been hiding in the shelter of the Whaler's Arms, next door. "Delhi?"

I jumped. "My Lord! What—"

"I was scared to go in the shop by myself," she confessed. "Marty's been known to eat his inferiors." She was wearing a blue sleeveless dress, makeup, and small pearl earrings. Her hair was tucked neatly behind her ears. *Miss Nebraska goes on a date.*

"Susie, you've got to get over that. Marty's no better than anyone else."

"If you say so."

The windows of the Old Frigate were still undecorated, but the "Closed" sign had been replaced by one that read, "Opening Soon."

Marty unlocked the door. "I don't drink," he barked when he saw the wine.

"More for us." I set the bottle down on the coffee table along with the white bakery box. Then I dropped my purse next to one of the wing chairs and sat down, leaning forward to unscrew the bottle cap. I poured wine into three cups anyway, as Susie undid the red-and-white bakery twine. Marty slouched into the other wing chair. Today he had on a royal blue T-shirt advertising "Buster's Vintage Mufflers" in white script.

"I guess you should find a new name for the shop," I said.

I could feel them both staring at me. I reached into the box and extracted a tiny éclair. "Shoot," I said. "I forgot napkins."

"You have something in mind?" Marty asked.

"Not me."

"We could always call it the New Shipwreck." Susie giggled, but subsided at his frown.

"The Re-Read Page?" I suggested.

Marty scowled. "Nothing cutesy."

"It might help if we knew what this shop would be

like," I said. "Margaret had a lot of common books, popular I mean, and people came in off the street to buy them." I turned to Marty. "Your books are on a different level. People aren't going to climb off the ferry and spend two hundred dollars on something 'collectible.'"

"Your point?"

"That it's not worth keeping a high-end shop open for hours and hours. Susie would be better off uploading the titles to the book services, and then shipping them."

"What's the point of having a shop then?"

Because you already own it? "Because it's a beautiful space. You could do a combination of our books. Susie's and some of mine in front, your collectible books protected. When collectors find out about your books, they *will* come. In the meantime, foot traffic will be able to find something to read."

Marty frowned at me through his black-framed glasses. "Why would I want to bring your books in?"

"Because if you don't, you're throwing your money away keeping an open shop in Port Lewis."

"Can I say something?" Susie asked timidly. "I'm good at uploading books to the Internet and mailing them. I could do that at the front counter and handle sales at the same time. We could put a couple of bookcases or tables outside with bargain books to pull people in—like they do at the Strand."

Marty looked as surprised as if Dr. Johnson's mythical dog had stood on its hind legs and discussed sales techniques.

"Susie's really fast," I agreed. "I could always decorate

the windows. I wouldn't be here much, but I could fill in when Susie couldn't be." I turned to her. "Would that work for you?"

"Sure. Paul won't be happy about weekends. But it's my life, too."

"Do you know how to describe books that *aren't* dreck?" Marty demanded.

I held my breath, but Susie laughed.

We thrashed out the details, including hours and Susie's salary. Even though I'd known how much Susie would be making, when I heard it again, my heart fluttered. Was I making a mistake by turning Marty down?

"I've got a ton of books warehoused," Marty warned Susie. "And it's still only an experiment. We'll give it six months."

I thought of the hours she would have to spend researching and describing his books, and decided it was no mistake at all.

CHAPTER FIFTY-FOUR

ON SUNDAY I printed out the Erikson book list and brought it along with my flash drive to Bianca. First I deleted Sonia's confession. There was no reason for anyone else to read it. Lynn had told the family everything, blaming herself more than she should have, and the story had been on the news.

Bianca met me at her cottage door, still too pale. She hadn't bothered to change out of a dark green bathrobe.

I sat down in what had now become my familiar spot on the quilted sofa, and took the cup of tea she handed me. "The final total for the books is high," I said. "You won't get quite that much, but it will be a nice amount."

"Good. We've decided to do things a little differently though."

I waited for her to tell me that my work had been irrelevant.

"We're still going to sell the books, some of them.

But first we'll go through and pick out the ones we want. Regan too. There's no point in selling off our heritage. When she came to see me in the hospital yesterday, we talked for hours. She told me that Gretchen had done the detail work on the illustrations." Bianca's expression was wondering. "I never even guessed. At least my father paid her well."

"What are you going to do now?"

She stared into her teacup moodily. "When I was in the hospital, I couldn't stand the pain at first so they gave me morphine. Lying in the dark, imagining if I had really died, I realized no one else would feel badly about it." She put up a hand to stop my protests. "I mean, I'm not special to anyone. Morgan and my father . . . but they're gone. Even you don't think I have a life."

"I never said that!"

"Maybe it's just the way you live compared to me. The way you do whatever you want. You still have all these things, all these people in your life. You're free—and I'm not."

I was stunned that she had been thinking anything like that. "Bianca, I'm just making it up as I go along."

"At least you're on a path."

"You can be too. Especially now, with Gretchen's money. What are the others going to do?"

"Claude's putting everything into his lab. He has an idea for something that might work this time. Lynn's just happy to stay on Long Island with her beloved shelter. My mother wants to go back to Charleston permanently. If she does, it will free Puck up to move to the Village.

Where else will they appreciate performance art? And being Nate Erikson's son will help him." She shrugged. "It's the way of the world."

"Rosa?"

"Oh, Rosa. She'll never come back here. She already has money of her own and with Gretchen's she can buy a house somewhere and have a real studio. And collect all the junk she wants."

"How do you feel about everything breaking up?" Thinking about the end of the dynasty made *me* sad. It was as if a beautiful piece of porcelain had been knocked off the mantel and shattered, with no one able to put it back together again.

"Nothing lasts forever. My father created this fairy tale world, we all believed in it, but he lived in fear that something would destroy it. It's ironic he was the one who did. Sonia—I can't even think about Sonia. I'm just thankful it wasn't one of *us*, we're crazy enough already."

I laughed. I wondered what would become of Adam's Revenge if everyone decided to leave, but I didn't ask. Early days yet, as Marselli would say.

Bianca set her teacup down and looked at me directly. It reminded me of the day I met her and she had asked me if I was satisfied with the books I had bought. "What are *you* going to do?"

"Me? Go back to the book business, I guess. Do the photos for your book if you still want them."

"I mean about Caitlin."

At that moment something surfaced in my mind, as

tangible as a notice slipped under a door. "I'm going to look for her. I hope Colin will too. It would change everything for us, for the whole family." Again, that bug on the windshield feeling. Exhilarating. Terrifying.

The way I seemed destined to live.

JUDI CULBERTSON draws on her experience as a used-and-rare-book dealer, social worker, and world traveler to create her bibliophile mysteries. No stranger to cemeteries, she also coauthored five illustrated guides with her husband, Tom Randall, starting with *Permanent Parisians*. She lives in Port Jefferson, New York, with her family.

Visit Judi online at www.judiculbertson.net.